CHARMS *and* CHIHUAHUAS

Familiar Spirits - Book 4

CHRISTINE POPE

This is a work of fiction. Names, characters, places, and incidents are either the product of the author's imagination or are used fictitiously. Any resemblance to actual events, places, organizations, or persons, whether living or dead, is entirely coincidental.

CHARMS AND CHIHUAHUAS

ISBN: 978-1-946435-72-9

Published by Dark Valentine Press

Cover design by Danielle Fine

Ebook formatting by Indie Author Services

Chapter 1

Speaking in Tongues

"Oh, hi, Charity," Tonya Willis called out as I stood in the produce section at our local supermarket, wondering whether any of the tomatoes on display were a likely candidate for a decent batch of salsa. Now that we were into the middle of September and the days were getting shorter...and cooler... I knew my boyfriend, Noah Jenkins, and I probably wouldn't have too many more chances for a backyard barbecue, and I wanted to make salsa while the sun shone.

So to speak.

"Hi, Tonya," I said in reply to her greeting, glad I sounded completely normal. It still felt awkward to bump into her like this, but enough time had passed since her unfortunate incident back in late

June that I had almost gotten used to the permanent alteration in her status.

Tonya had been a prominent part of our coven here in Salem...right up until the time I discovered she was also secretly the head of another coven in the neighboring town of Marblehead, where she'd run the group with an iron fist and had basically told the other witches in her coven if and when they could have children...and who with. Most likely, neither I nor my fellow Salem witches would have discovered her terrible lie...if it hadn't been for the way the dark magic she used to enforce her edicts ended up accidentally killing one of her own coven's witches.

She'd also been involved in some nasty blackmail on the side, and we'd collectively decided her crimes were too terrible to allow her to continue wielding so much power. That was why Elise Figg, a member of my coven who dabbled in much darker magic than the rest of us, was the one who destroyed Tonya's pineal gland, rendering her unable to use any of her powers.

With her magic gone, Tonya had absolutely no recollection of her time in our coven, or the coven in Marblehead. She thought she was an ordinary person with ordinary friends, which turned out to be handy for everyone concerned, because we could pretend there was nothing unusual about any of us and that we knew her simply because we'd all lived in Salem for most of our lives.

"How's that handsome boyfriend of yours?" she asked, and I was glad to give her a perfectly natural smile in reply.

"Oh, Noah's fine," I said. "We're planning a barbecue for tomorrow, and that's why I'm thinking about making salsa."

Tonya's gaze flickered upward, as if speculating on the current condition of the skies above the roof of our local Market Basket. I'd stopped there on my way home from Full Moon Apothecary, the store I operated in downtown Salem, figuring I'd pick up a few supplies. Noah was away at a convention in Boston, but he'd be back late Sunday, which was why we'd set up the barbecue for tomorrow afternoon rather than today.

"Good thing you're planning to do your outdoor activities this weekend," Tonya informed me. "I saw on the news that it's supposed to turn rainy on Monday."

I hadn't heard that, but then, most witches really didn't require forecasters to let them know what the weather was going to be like. A sniff of the breeze could tell us rain was on the way, just as some sixth sense always warned us in advance when we were going to have a hard freeze.

Obviously, I couldn't mention anything about my supernatural weather sense to Tonya, though, since every single witch in our coven had to do her best to pretend there was nothing out of the ordinary about any of us. Instead, I assumed what I hoped was an interested expression and said, "Oh, really? That's good to know. I just figured it would be fun to be outside one last time before fall really arrived."

"You definitely chose the right weekend for it," she said. "Well, I'll let you get back to your shopping. Say hi to your mother for me."

I promised I would, and Tonya rolled her cart away from the produce section, looking as though she was headed for the meat department. That was my next destination, but I thought I'd linger here for a while until the coast was clear.

Having to act normal could be exhausting when you were anything but.

It felt a little strange to be home alone on a Saturday night, since usually I would go to Noah's or he would come to my place, depending on what we felt like doing on any particular day. Then again, I wasn't truly alone, not when I had Milo with me. I'd adopted the cocker spaniel after his witch mistress was murdered back in late May, and although I couldn't say he was exactly my familiar, he was definitely one of the closest friends I had in the world.

I'd made my mother's yummy, super comfort food-y mac and cheese for dinner, and because I spoiled Milo without a single twinge of regret, I put down my bowl for him to lick after I was done.

"Don't you dare tell Noah I did this," I warned the dog, whose feathered tail swished back and forth with joy as he slurped up any of the milk and cheese mixture that remained in the bowl.

"I can't tell him anything," Milo said mildly. "He wouldn't understand me."

I'd intended my comment as a joke, but Milo, as with most dogs, tended to take people's comments literally. It was true that Noah wouldn't be able to understand a single word Milo said—regular humans or even almost all witches wouldn't have understood him, either.

But I had the rare gift of being able to understand familiars' speech, which was why I was unofficially known as the "familiar whisperer" in the witch community. From time to time, a witch might bring her companion animal to me if she was having trouble with them, and by having them here at my house, I was able to give both the witch and her familiar a little break from one another and also—with any luck—get to the bottom of what was causing their issues. Almost always, they were able to return home to enjoy an improved relationship with their mistresses.

Well, unless they had the bad luck to get murdered, like Darla Fitzgerald, Milo's former witch.

That was a very rare occurrence, luckily, and the last two familiars I'd had in my care had gone home to their mistresses without too much incident. Or rather, while there might have been murder involved, their witches had managed to escape all the ugliness unscathed.

Several months had passed since Lionel the hedgehog had stayed with me, and his mistress, Sela Warren, seemed to have settled down just fine with her new husband. Then again, since Sela was one of the unfortunate witches who'd had Tonya as her coven leader...and had also lost her sister due to Tonya's terrible magic...I had to believe she was living her best life now that she no longer had to worry about Tonya Willis's horrible kind of interference.

It often happened this way, that I'd have large gaps in between watching familiars. To be honest, I was just fine with the downtime, especially considering all the skullduggery that had interrupted my life last summer. A quiet, uneventful autumn would be nice—or at least, as uneventful as things ever were in Salem in the fall, since it was our busiest tourist season and the pace at my shop would be lively pretty much from the time I opened at ten to when I closed up at five.

That was a regular kind of busyness, though, one I welcomed, because those hectic days in late September and all through October were what helped sustain me during the slow winter months when tourism dropped off hugely before things started to pick up sometime in May. Yes, I had my regulars here in Salem, but their business on its own wouldn't have been enough to sustain the store without the way I always made sure to sock away a bunch of cash the preceding autumn.

"Well, he wouldn't understand you word for word," I told Milo. "But I think Noah's still pretty good at picking up a lot of what you mean despite that."

The dog turned away from the bowl, which had been pretty much licked clean by that point, and came over so he could jump up next to me on the couch. Because I'd been eating alone, I hadn't seen the point in sitting down at the dining room table and had instead brought my food into the living room and eaten there, with the TV on in the background. I hadn't been paying much attention to the show, but it was still nice to have it playing anyway, keeping me company.

"Noah is very good at that," Milo said. "Better than any other human I've ever met." He paused there, looking up at me with inquisitive brown eyes. "You miss him, don't you?"

"Yes," I replied, since it was only the truth. "But he'll be back tomorrow, and he was only away for three days."

Three days that had felt like an eternity, even though I'd done my best to tell myself it was silly to get so worked up about Noah's absence when we'd only been dating for about four months. Deep down, however, I knew things were serious between us. He'd taken me to meet his parents over Labor Day weekend, and I'd finally bitten the bullet and had him meet my mother, who, thank God, had been on her best behavior. Not that she would have ever done anything to jeopardize my relationship with Noah, only that she could sometimes be a little overwhelming in large doses.

But he'd taken the encounter in stride—we'd met for a late afternoon nosh at Tea & Sympathy, the shop my friend Stella owned—and hadn't shown any signs of wanting to dump me after our little meeting. No, he'd only said my mother was a lot of fun and that he hoped we could get together again sometime in the near future.

Some men might have lied about something like that, but in Noah's case, I knew he was only telling me the honest truth.

Despite all this positive forward motion, though, I hadn't yet gotten the courage to tell him the truth about me...and my mother, and in fact, all the women who were my closest friends. Since neither Noah nor I had yet uttered the "L-word" to each other, it wasn't too hard to convince myself that we weren't at a point in our relationship where I felt comfortable letting him know I was a witch. I had to be absolutely, positively sure he was the only man in the world for me...and I was the only woman in the world for him...before I could take such a huge step.

And as much as I missed Noah now, I doubted I would say anything on the subject to him when we met tomorrow.

As promised, the day was gorgeous, with sapphire-hued skies and just a few clouds floating by to give the weather some dimension. Noah had texted to let me know he was on his way home from Boston and that we could still meet at his house at five, so I went ahead and whipped up the salsa and stored it in a bowl with a sealing lid, then placed it in the fridge next to the steaks I'd been marinating all night. He'd protested that he could take care of the main course, but I'd only told him he shouldn't have to do much work since he'd been away these past three days.

Milo had sniffed around the kitchen but had

mostly stayed out from underfoot, which was about the best I could hope for. And when four forty-five rolled around, I stowed everything in a reusable shopping bag and headed out to my ancient Land Rover, the dog trotting at my heels. He almost always came along if we were eating in, and only stayed behind on those occasions when Noah's and my plans involved eating indoors at a sit-down restaurant that didn't allow dogs.

Not for the first time, I reflected how lucky I was that I'd gotten involved with someone who loved animals and didn't see anything strange about the way Milo and I were almost joined at the hip. Ours wasn't a true witch/familiar relationship, but it came close enough, and after going through the trauma of losing his mistress, he needed someone who would be close by and give him the love and attention he needed. True, he stayed home when I went to work, but my house had a doggy door and a big backyard that offered plenty of diversions during the time I was gone, and he'd assured me he was fine with the setup.

Noah answered the door almost as soon as I knocked, telling me he must have been missing me just as badly as I was missing him. The kiss he gave me after I came inside only confirmed my theory, a warm, welcome kiss that made me a little weak in the knees...and very, very glad that I didn't have to work the next day so I could be up until all hours tonight.

Well, not all hours, probably, because although my shop was closed on Sundays and Mondays, Noah would still have to be at the clinic.

Still, I was resolved to enjoy the evening, even if it ended with me going home rather than staying the night. I'd take my cues from him and see what he wanted to do.

Right now, however, the order of the day was to unpack the goodies I'd brought and head outside to the patio, where the sun was warm even if the breeze felt cooler than I'd expected, telling me the rain Tonya had warned me about was probably on the way sometime during the overnight hours. For now, though, Noah and I could enjoy our chips and salsa and wine, and I'd worry about the storm when it got here.

"How was the conference?" I asked after we'd seated ourselves at the table on the patio and clinked our glasses together to celebrate our reunion.

"It was fine," he said. "Honestly, I would rather have skipped it, but Alex Hawthorne, the vet I used to work for in Boston, was there, and it was a chance to get together and catch up. I'm just glad no emergencies cropped up while I was gone. People could have gone to Dr. Crowne's clinic instead, but I wanted to avoid that if possible."

Yes, that was the hard part about being in a profession where your clients relied on you for life-and-death matters. People could survive if I closed the shop down for a few days...well, unless they forgot to stock up on their insomnia elixir beforehand...but if your dog came down with a weird bout of vomiting or your kitty was hit by a car, you needed to know someone would be there to help right away.

"I'm glad everything was quiet here," I said. "And I hope you don't have any surgeries scheduled for first thing tomorrow morning."

Across the table, Noah's bright blue eyes glinted at me. Those eyes had been the first thing I noticed about him, almost of laser-beam clarity, although once I stopped looking at his eyes, I'd noted that his wavy brown hair, regular features, and athletic physique weren't too bad, either.

"No surgeries until ten," he said. "And I told my staff I might not be in until nine, so...."

No need to finish the sentence; I knew exactly what he was hinting at.

Good thing we kept some kibble for Milo here...not to mention the drawer in Noah's bedroom that had some of my extra underwear and a change of clothes, just in case. My spare toothbrush had taken up permanent residence at the house months before.

"I like a man who thinks ahead," I said, and he chuckled.

"You were all I was thinking about while I was gone."

From a couple of the guys I'd dated in the past, those words might have been just a little creepy. Coming from Noah, though, they were only more confirmation that things were serious between us, a lot more serious than I might have wanted to acknowledge.

"Well, I'll admit I pondered this salsa a bit," I replied, taking care to keep my tone light. "Otherwise, though...."

Once again, his eyes met mine. Mouth turning up slightly at the corners, he said, "It's still early. Want to kill some time before we put those steaks on the grill?"

I set down my glass of wine. "Thought you'd never ask."

By that point, I'd spent so many nights at Noah's house that there really wasn't a "walk of shame" the next morning. We shared some coffee and toast, and then I gathered up Milo so I could head home and get showered and ready to start my day.

Which, admittedly, would be a quiet one. On my

days off, I generally puttered around the house, took Milo for long walks if the weather allowed, and maybe put together a few elixirs and tinctures if I was running low on a particular type at my store. Noah and I texted when we could, but since he'd been away for several days and had a very busy schedule lined up, I honestly hadn't expected to hear from him until late in the afternoon, and maybe not even then.

That was why, just after I'd finished putting my lunch plate away in the dishwasher, I was surprised to get a text from Noah.

My neighbor brought in a chihuahua she found wandering near Collins Cove Park. No one there claimed her as theirs, and she isn't chipped. Would you mind fostering her for a couple of days while I try to track down the owner?

It made sense Noah would reach out to me for help, since he knew I fostered animals. He couldn't keep the dog at his house because it was a rental and his lease wouldn't allow him to have a pet. We'd been stretching the letter of the lease just by having Milo stay over, but we figured we were still technically not breaking any rules since he was my dog and not Noah's.

And because Milo loved all animals and was always happy to have a four-legged friend, if even for a few days, I didn't hesitate to reply.

Sure. I can be there in about fifteen minutes.

Thank you so much!

I sent him a smiley emoji, then set the phone down on the countertop so I could close up the dishwasher. Once I was done with that, I went out to the living room, where Milo was curled up on his favorite rug in front of the hearth.

"Noah just asked if we could host a lost dog for a couple of days," I said. "You okay with that?"

"Sure," Mile responded. "It won't be quite the same as having another familiar here, but I'll do my best to make them feel at home."

True, familiars could talk to other familiars, but they didn't have that same facility when it came to regular animals. Milo was such a sweet soul, though, that I knew he wouldn't hold the difference over our foster dog's head.

"I know you will," I said. "I'm just going to go pick up the dog and will be right back. I shouldn't be gone for more than twenty minutes."

"I'll be here," Milo promised.

I patted him on the head, told him he was a good boy, and headed out to the garage to get into my SUV. As I went, a few spatters of rain hit my head, letting me know the clouds that had been threatening all morning had finally decided to get on with it already.

Well, by this point in our relationship, Noah should be used enough to the way my flaming red hair frizzed at the slightest provocation that I wouldn't let myself worry about it.

His clinic was about ten minutes away from my house. Luckily, it was still early enough in the afternoon that I didn't have to worry about getting delayed by kids in crosswalks or armies of moms in SUVs picking their children up from school, a hazard I'd run into on more than one occasion while coming and going from the clinic.

Now, though, I drove into the parking lot without incident and walked right in the front door. By that point, everyone who worked there knew me well enough that I didn't have to do anything except smile and wave.

Courtney, the vet assistant who usually manned the front desk, acknowledged me with an answering smile. "Noah's in exam room two," she said. "Thanks so much for taking that poor little dog."

"Is she okay?" I asked, and Courtney nodded.

"Looks like it," she replied. "Just scared, I think."

That didn't surprise me too much. The world was a big and scary enough place even when you weren't the size of a chihuahua.

Even though I knew Noah was expecting me, I still knocked on the door of the second exam room, just to be safe. He opened it immediately, one arm cradling a darling little long-haired chihuahua with striking tricolor markings.

"Oh, she's adorable!" I exclaimed, and he smiled.

"Yes, she's a sweet girl," he said. "I'm really surprised she isn't microchipped, since she otherwise looks well cared for."

"No collar?"

He shook his head, even as his strong, sensitive fingers kept stroking the base of the little dog's oversized ears. She leaned into him, giving weight, obviously charmed by the attention. "No collar. Nothing to say where she came from or who she belongs to. And I really appreciate you taking her at such short notice like this."

"It's not a problem at all," I assured him. "I've got lots of room. And you know Milo loves all other dogs."

Because Noah and I had taken Milo for plenty of walks, he knew this was the simple truth. Being a familiar didn't exempt my cocker spaniel from wanting to touch noses...and other parts of his anatomy...with the various dogs we met while strolling through the neighborhood. Also, he was fiercely protective and would make sure no harm came to this little lost girl while she was in my care.

The brilliant smile I received in reply to that comment was confirmation enough. "Yes, Milo is great," Noah replied. "Courtney will set you up with some food for small dogs—I know what you feed Milo is going to be too much for this girl. I wish I could spend more time with the two of you, but I've got someone coming in at one-thirty."

"It's fine," I said quickly. While I also wished I could linger, I knew Noah had other patients he needed to take care of. "How about you come by after work and we can order some pizza?"

"Sounds great," he replied at once. "I have a late appointment at five-thirty, but I'll come over after that."

We sealed the deal with a kiss—a quick one that wouldn't seem too off-putting to our tiny charge. He handed over the dog, who felt like a featherweight in my arms after dealing with Milo those times I had to lug him in and out of the bathtub. She seemed to understand she was with someone who cared, because she immediately burrowed into me, her tiny snout buried between my arm and my body.

"I think she likes you," Noah remarked.

"She seems like a real sweetie," I replied.

He reached out to squeeze my hand, but then let go so I could head out of the exam room and up to the front desk, where Courtney got out a sample-size bag of Science Diet and handed it over. I doubted the bag contained enough to feed the dog for more than two or three days at the most, but that was all right. By that point, either we would have figured out who her owner was, or I would have found the time to go to the pet store and get her a more adequate supply of food.

I always kept a towel in the back seat of my Land Rover in case Milo had muddy paws, and now I grabbed it and sort of smooshed it into an impromptu bed on the front seat so I could put the chihuahua there for the ride home. She understood at once and climbed onto the towel, nudging it with her tiny nose so it lay more to her specifications.

While she was occupied, I went around to the driver's side of the SUV and climbed behind the wheel, then backed out of the space where I was parked and turned onto Fort Avenue so I could head home.

"Don't worry," I told the dog once we were up to speed. "You're going to come stay at my house for a little while, and then as soon as we figure out who you really belong to, we'll take you home."

"Oh, I'm not worried," the dog said in a high-pitched little voice, and I barely kept myself from slamming on the brakes in surprise. Good thing there weren't any cars in our immediate vicinity.

The dog Noah had rescued was a familiar? But no witch would ever let her familiar out of her sight...or at least, she definitely wouldn't allow her animal companion to wander around in a public park without a collar and tag, let alone no microchip. Every case was different because so many different types of animals served as familiars, but when the familiar in question was a dog or cat, the witch who owned them would certainly follow the usual protocols by having all their shots in order, a license if necessary, and a microchip.

I managed to recover myself enough to ask, "What were you doing in that park? Who's your witch?"

The dog blinked her big brown eyes. They were darker than Milo's, nearly black, surrounded by black fur that stood out against the light brown of the rest of her face, giving her the impression of wearing a mask. "My witch?" she said, sounding confused.

"Well, you're talking to me," I said. "That means you must be a familiar."

A little shake, and the dog responded, "I'm not a familiar."

All right, it was my turn to be befuddled. "But the only animals who can talk are familiars."

She blinked. "I only started talking the day before yesterday."

As Alice in Wonderland might have said, curiouser and curiouser. True, there were spells that could make animals speak, but they were very difficult to cast and in general only lasted for a short time. A witch would only use such a spell if there was a particular piece of information she needed, such as asking a woodland creature if they'd seen someone pass their way. It wasn't as if we went around enchanting animals so we'd have someone to talk to about our love lives.

But if the little chihuahua was telling the truth...and I had no reason to believe she wasn't, since dogs tended to be very honest creatures...then the spell that was allowing us to hold this conversation had been in place for several days.

"Who cast the spell on you?"

Another blink. "Someone cast a spell?"

She seemed genuinely perplexed, so I didn't think she was being obtuse on purpose. From what I could tell, whoever had placed this enchantment on the dog had done so secretly, so not even the subject of the spell knew what was going on. It was entirely possible the chihuahua's owner wasn't a witch at all.

Grimly, I pressed my foot on the accelerator, wanting nothing more than to get home as fast as possible.

One way or another, I needed to get to the bottom of this.

Chapter 2

Lexi Lexicon

"She's definitely not a familiar," Milo announced after touching noses with the chihuahua and getting a whiff of her scent.

"I already told her that," the little dog said, now sounding almost annoyed.

All right, we'd start from the beginning. "What's your name?"

"Lexi," she replied. Her expression appeared a little less strained, as if she was relieved that I'd asked such an innocuous question.

"Did you talk to anyone at the vet clinic?"

She gave another of those shakes, which I guessed was her way of processing something she didn't quite understand. "I tried to, but no one could understand me," she said. "They just petted me and told me I was okay and that they were going to figure out where I lived as soon as they could." A pause, and her pert little nose twitched. "I don't think it was anywhere around here, though. It doesn't smell right."

Should I be offended? My house was always kept clean, but I had to admit some of the brews I concocted for sale at my shop could get a little pungent before they were safely stored in a bottle.

Milo, however, was quicker on the uptake than I, probably because he also possessed a sensitive dog's nose and had a better idea of what Lexi might be smelling at the moment. "Your house wasn't by the ocean?"

"Oh, is that what that scent is?" she replied. "That salty smell?"

The cocker spaniel nodded.

"Then no," she said. "We weren't by the ocean. We had lots of trees around our house."

Which didn't narrow things down very much, since there were plenty of places in the inland parts of my home state that were heavily wooded. But at least it was a data point, if not a super-helpful one. Also, I found it interesting that Lexi could talk to me but not to Noah or Courtney or anyone else at the vet clinic. Did that mean the little dog could only speak to me because of my gift for communicating with familiars, or was it more because I was a witch?

That particular question shouldn't be too difficult to answer, although I had a few more things I wanted to ask first.

"Who's your owner?"

Lexi tilted her head to one side. "Milton."

Her owner was a man? For some reason, I'd just expected them to be a woman...in particular, a witch. But if Lexi was owned by a man named Milton, then who had cast the spell on the dog?

"Do you know who made you talk?" I asked.

That question earned me a wrinkled nose. "No. I just woke up the day before yesterday and had all these words come out. I don't even remember thinking in words like this before."

No, she probably wouldn't have, if she really had started out as an ordinary dog. Familiars' thought processes were much more human, most likely because they had to communicate with their witches on a daily basis.

As to how someone could have cast a spell on Lexi without her even knowing what had happened, the situation wasn't as strange as one might think. Not all spells required the witch working the enchantment to be in the same room as their subject. All she would have needed was some of Lexi's fur, which, considering how luxurious it was, most likely had been shed all over her neighborhood. Anyone who really wanted to make her the focus of a spell wouldn't have had too hard a time gathering the components they needed.

Of course, that particular fact made me circle back to why someone would want to make Lexi talk in the first place. She was an adorable little thing, but so far she hadn't offered any pearls of wisdom that would have made me think she was hiding some sort of important secret.

Milo had remained sitting off to one side, watching the exchange, but now he spoke up. "Did you notice anyone strange near your house, anyone who shouldn't have been there?"

Lexi's pert black nose wrinkled again. "I don't think so," she replied. "That is, I didn't see anyone out walking their dogs or leaving for their job or anything like that who wasn't a person I hadn't seen lots of times before."

My dog's ears drooped a little at that reply. I could tell he'd been hoping his line of questioning might have yielded better fruit.

Still, that didn't mean Lexi didn't have a witch who lived in her neighborhood, someone everybody else thought was just a regular woman. We witches had to hide who we were; it wasn't as if we were worried about being burned at the stake or anything like that, but at the same time, we felt it much safer for the world to go on believing magic wasn't real. I thought it very possible that someone across the street or even next door was a witch, and for whatever reason, she'd decided it was a good idea to make Lexi talk.

Of course, what we really needed to nail down was where exactly the little dog had come from. Since she'd said she couldn't smell the ocean from her house, I knew the place had to be located somewhere inland. Massachusetts wasn't a big state, but there were still quite a few towns that had twenty miles or more between them and the coast, which meant narrowing things to a list of four or five likely suspects might be more difficult than I thought.

Still, I needed to try.

"Can you tell me anything about the neighborhood where you lived?" I asked. "You said there were lots of trees. Were the houses close together, or did they sit on bigger plots of land?"

"Big pieces of land," Lexi replied promptly. "There were only three houses on my street."

Well, that helped a little. I was lucky that my vintage house sat on nearly an acre, but a lot of neighborhoods in Salem had the homes packed pretty tightly together because the land here was so valuable. It was the same story in many places in my home state, but once you got farther inland where people still had farms and weren't trying to wring the most out of every spare inch of real estate, there were homes that sat on plots of three or more acres.

I wracked my brains, trying to remember which towns I'd been to that more or less matched Lexi's description, but the problem was, lots of inland Massachusetts was like that. And for all I knew, the little dog wasn't from here at all, but neighboring New Hampshire or Connecticut, which meant trying to discover where she'd come from would be nearly impossible.

Of course, that begged the question as to why someone would dump Lexi at a park in Salem when she'd come from a neighboring state...unless whoever had left her there had wanted to make sure she was very far from home.

"Do you remember if someone drove you a long way to get to that park where you were found?"

Lexi's luxurious feathery tail thumped against the floor, although I got the feeling she hadn't been wagging it because she was happy, but more because she knew there was a hole in her memory she couldn't explain.

"I don't know how I got there," she said, confirming my suspicions. "It felt like I took a long nap, and then when I woke up, I was at that park under a tree. It looked like a nice place, so I decided to explore it. That was when that lady found me and took me to the vet." The dog's head tilted to the side, and she added, sounding annoyed, "I don't know why she would do something like that. I'm not sick, and I wasn't bothering anyone."

"I think it's because she was worried you were there all by yourself," I said gently. "The lady brings her own dogs to Noah's clinic, so she knew he'd be able to figure out what to do. And I said I'd watch you because I foster animals all the time."

At those words, Lexi looked over at Milo. "Is she fostering you?"

"No," he said. "Charity adopted me after my mistress died. But she does have lots of animals coming through here."

Lexi didn't look too thrilled by that comment. Was she worried someone was about to drop off a Great Dane at my front door?

Maybe, which meant I needed to put her fears to rest as best I could.

"Well, 'lots' might be a slight exaggeration," I said. "We haven't had a foster here for almost two months. But I'm sure that's why Noah got in touch with me—he thought you'd be better off here than at the animal shelter."

Was that the slightest flicker of alarm in the chihuahua's big dark eyes?

"I definitely don't want to go *there,*" she said, her tone emphatic.

"I know," I replied. "Which is why you're here with me. I'll take care of you until we can get all this figured out." I paused there and glanced over at Milo. "Milo, why don't you take Lexi out to see the backyard? She might need to go."

He seemed all too happy to comply with my

request, saying, "Yes, it's a good backyard. You'll like it. Follow me."

The two of them trotted out of the living room, something about Lexi's happy little almost-prance telling me she was very glad to go outside and enjoy the fresh air instead of having me grill her about topics she didn't know. And I was fine with giving her a break...but I knew I couldn't stop here.

No, I needed to bring in an expert.

"It's quite a difficult spell," Grace Bowersby, my coven's resident witchy historian, said. She was looking slightly flummoxed after hearing Lexi speak, although she gave the little dog a friendly smile and was obviously doing her best not to say anything that might alarm my newest charge.

I thought I could understand why Grace was having a hard time with this, if only because she was used to hearing only her rat familiar Jonas speak and no other animals, while I had the ability to talk to all of them.

Well, not every animal. I definitely hadn't sat down with my neighbor's cat Moopsie to get her dish on the neighborhood and its various doings. Then again, Moopsie seemed more interested in chasing down any mice or rats in the area than having a heart-to-heart, so I wasn't sure she'd have much to say to me even if I could talk to regular animals.

"But not impossible," I replied, and Grace shook her head.

"No, not at all," she said. "Do you have any idea why someone would want to do such a thing to this dog?"

"Absolutely none," I replied. "I think she's from somewhere inland, but that's about all I have to go on at the moment. She definitely hasn't said anything that makes me think she's hiding some kind of secret."

"'Inland,'" Grave repeated in musing tones. "Then I doubt anyone who cast this spell has anything to do with our coven."

Thank God. After dealing with Tonya Willis's treachery and its unpleasant aftermath, I really didn't want to entertain the idea that someone else in our witchy group might be hiding some deep, dark secrets of her own.

"Is there any way to detect who did cast the spell?" I asked next.

Grace's rose-lipsticked mouth pursed. As usual, she wore colors that were bright bordering on garish, today a short-sleeved cobalt blue sweater and kelly green pants embroidered with little blue whales. Not for the first time, I thought there was no way anyone in the world would look at her and think she was a witch.

And I guessed that was precisely the point.

"Not really," she replied in answer to my question. "Sometimes I can detect a spell cast by someone in our coven, just because I know everyone so well and can recognize the resonance of their magic, for lack of a better term. But because this enchantment must have been created by a witch who isn't one of us, there's no way for me to trace it back to her. You'd be better off attempting a scrying and seeing if it will show you anything of use."

The thought had already crossed my mind, but I'd decided to have Grace weigh in first and provide me with her perspective on the situation. Besides, although scrying had helped me in the past, it wasn't one of my magical strengths and I never knew whether it was going to actually work at any given time.

"That's my next step," I said.

"Good. I will say that I don't detect any traces of dark magic around the dog, nothing that would make me think this is anything but a simple spell to allow her to speak. It is interesting that it's lasted so long, though."

Again, pretty much what I'd thought. All I could do was hope the enchantment would continue to work, because if Lexi lost her power of speech any time soon, it would be that much more difficult to figure out where she'd come from... and why.

"But I need to get home," Grace went on. "Cailie's bringing Olivia over for me to watch so she can go to her doctor's appointment. Number two will be here any day."

Cailie was Grace's daughter and Olivia was her granddaughter. However, because Cailie had moved to Seabrook after she got married, she'd joined the local coven there rather than remaining part of ours. Despite that, she wanted the same doctor who'd delivered her and her first child to take care of her during this second pregnancy, which was why she was now back in town.

I still found it a little surprising that Cailie was going for baby number two, just because a lot of witches stopped after having their first daughter, figuring one girl would be enough to ensure the continuation of their line. We never had boys because—as I'd learned quite recently—magic somehow got distorted in a person with a Y-chromosome, became something dark and deadly.

"Then I won't keep you," I said quickly. The last thing I wanted was to make Grace late to watch her granddaughter. "I just appreciate you coming by."

"Oh, it's no problem," she assured me. "To be

honest, I find this whole situation fascinating. Just let me know what you find out."

I promised her I would, then walked her to the door and waved goodbye as she descended the front steps. Once I turned around, though, it was to find both Lexi and Milo watching me with matching quizzical expressions.

"She didn't seem to know very much," Lexi remarked.

"Well, she's never encountered anything like this before," I said, even as I wondered if all chihuahuas were judge-y, or just this particular specimen. "But she did confirm that she could hear and understand you, which tells me whoever cast the spell, they wanted to make sure you could communicate only with witches and not regular people. I guess I'm just trying to figure out why."

Lexi reached up with her hind foot to scratch behind one ear. "Maybe whoever cast the spell told me something that I'm supposed to tell another witch."

Her theory sounded like a logical enough assumption...except for the part where the little dog hadn't yet given me a single piece of truly useful information, and it didn't seem as though she planned to do so any time soon.

"Can you think of anything you know that you'd like to tell me?" I asked, even as I guessed the answer would be a big no.

Before Lexi could reply, though, Milo ventured, "Maybe that's another part of the spell. Do you think the spell caster told Lexi something important, but she locked it behind another kind of spell that needs to be broken first before she can reveal what she knows?"

I'd never heard of such a thing, which didn't mean a lot. Unlike Grace, I didn't have much interest in witch history, and unlike some other members of our coven—such as Elise Figg, who definitely enjoyed delving into the more arcane forms of the magical arts—I didn't have a lot of time for experimentation. No, I was just fine with following the tried and true spells and enchantments that would help me with my everyday life, and leaving the crazy stuff to other people.

"That's very good thinking, Milo," I told him, and his feathery golden-brown tail wagged at hearing the praise. "The problem is, even if someone did cast that kind of spell on Lexi, I'm not sure how I can break it."

Both dogs didn't appear too happy to hear my comment, but that didn't keep Lexi from saying, "But maybe someone else in your coven would be able to."

"Maybe," I allowed. It was true that Elise Figg might be able to help, but I didn't really like the idea of reaching out to her for assistance. She'd never done anything to harm me—or anyone in our coven—but I couldn't forget how she'd been blackmailed into putting a hex on Sela Warren's hedgehog and had calmly recited the spell that had destroyed Tonya Willis's pineal gland. A just punishment in the latter case, I supposed, and yet I still didn't like the idea of being beholden to someone who didn't have a problem using that kind of magic.

Only as a last resort, I told myself.

In the meantime, I had one more thing I could try.

Milo and Lexi returned to the backyard to do more exploring, which meant I had some uninterrupted time to attempt a scrying spell. I got down the silver basin I used for this kind of magic from its shelf in the cupboard and set it on the kitchen table before heading into the pantry so I could fetch one of the big jugs of moon water I'd prepared during the last full moon. While I usually didn't need that much, I'd gotten caught with my pants down the last time I'd had to perform a scrying and had been forced to use distilled water, and ever since then, I'd made sure to set out two large containers of water to get charged by moonlight.

As I poured some water into the silver basin, I did my best to remain focused on exactly what I wanted the scrying to show me—namely, the person who'd cast the spell on Lexi. This sort of enchantment wouldn't provide a lot of information as to exactly why they'd felt compelled to perform this kind of magic, but if I could even get a face—heck, a house number—I'd feel as if I'd made at least a little progress.

Now, time to see just what I could discover.

Whispers of truth now softly unfurl,

Reveal the caster of words on this tiny girl.

From silence to speech, the transformation was made,

Show the witch's face lest their identity fade.

Small ripples moved across the surface of the scrying mirror and I held my breath, wondering if those ripples would resolve into an actual scene or whether they'd simply dissipate as they had on several other occasions when I'd attempted this kind of magic. As I'd told Grace, sometimes I had success with this sort of thing, and sometimes I didn't. I had no idea whether it was luck or chance or simply the phase of the moon, because there didn't seem to be much rhyme or reason to it otherwise.

But then the surface of the water stilled, and a blurry image began to appear in it, growing slowly sharper. It showed me the back of a woman wearing black, her dark hair pulled into a ponytail that hung halfway to her waist. She was bending over a sleeping Lexi, who looked as if she lay in her bed at home. Although I couldn't see much, I could at least tell the floor was dark wood and that the bed had been placed up against a wall near a window, where light flooded in and showed a flutter of green leaves, maybe oak, maybe birch.

Well, that was something, but since I'd specifically asked the spell to reveal the face of the witch who'd placed the enchantment on Lexi, I was a little annoyed to only see the woman's back and nothing else. Yes, her hair was dark brown and longish, but because millions of other women had hair basically just like that, I didn't think such a small clue was going to help me very much.

Since I'd faced similar bumps in the road when attempting this sort of spell in the past, I wasn't going to allow myself to be too dismayed. I'd just have to try again and hope for a better result.

Whisper of tongues, silent and small,
Reveal to us the caster's call.
From shadows deep to light of day,
Show the hand that spoke this way.

. . .

The image the scrying mirror had shown me of the witch leaning over Lexi's bed disappeared, and I held my breath. At best, I had one more try after this, since I'd learned long ago that I couldn't keep beating away at the same question over and over again once the mirror had decided it wasn't in the mood to be helpful.

A shiver of the water, and I saw the witch again, this time walking down what looked like a trail through the woods, with oaks and elms and white pine crowding on all sides. It was a very pretty scene, but since all it showed me was her back again, it wasn't of any more use than the one I'd seen a moment earlier. Okay, at least this time I could tell she was wearing a skirt that hit her at mid-calf and she had on a pair of lace-up black boots, but considering half the witches of my acquaintance—and all the women in Salem who liked to play at being a witch but who lacked a single ounce of magic—owned similar footwear, again, I didn't see how this could narrow things down at all.

Time to try something a little different.

Whiskers wander, paws so small,
Lead us to where the lost one calls.
Through streets and shadows, make it known,
Reveal the place this pup calls home.

Once again, the water shimmered, then became calm again. On its surface, the image of a large white-painted house surrounded by trees took shape, with a path of neat pavers going to the front door and what I thought might be a two-car garage off to one side, with a long, winding driveway that led up to it.

Eyes narrowing, I leaned down toward the image, hoping I could make out a street number somewhere on the house. Unfortunately, the reflection in the mirror was from far enough away that I couldn't see anything useful, not even a car parked in the driveway. And since Massachusetts positively teemed with white-painted houses set back amongst trees, I didn't know whether this one data point was going to help me very much. True, the house had pale gray trim, but that was a popular exterior paint combo in this part of the world, and again, didn't provide nearly enough unique detail to go on.

However, I wasn't going to give up that easily. I'd learned a while back that the images a scrying mirror showed were real, and if I could grab a shot of one with my phone before the image faded away, then I'd have something I could show someone...or, as I planned to do in this case, I'd have a photo I could upload to Google's image search to see if it could help me narrow things down.

My phone sat on the kitchen counter nearby,

and I grabbed it and aimed it at the bowl, then took several quick snaps in succession. Not a moment too soon, because just as I began to lower the phone, the water inside the silver bowl shimmered and went dark.

I took a look at the photos I'd taken, selected the sharpest one, and then headed out to the backyard. It couldn't hurt to have Lexi confirm it really was her house in the image before I started trying to track it down online.

The two dogs were lying on a sunny patch of grass not too far from the back door. Off to one side was the herb garden, but it seemed clear they hadn't been interested in that and were much happier taking advantage of the unusually mild day.

However, as soon as they heard me descend the back stairs, they blinked awake and got to their feet.

"Have a nice nap?" I asked as Lexi gave a shake that went all the way from her pert little nose to the waving black flag of her tail.

"Yes," she said. "The sun is nice out here. Of course, you don't have as much open space as there is in my own yard, but it's still good for sleeping."

Somehow, I managed to repress the smile that threatened to tug at my lips. If the big white house I'd seen in the vision really was where Lexi lived, then I had to admit she had me beat. I loved my home, loved that it was more than a hundred and fifty years old and had a certain funkiness due to the way it had been added on to without much rhyme or reason over the years, but I knew it couldn't compare to a four-thousand-square-foot almost-mansion out in the countryside, especially one that looked as if it sat on at least three or four acres, maybe more.

"I'm glad to hear that," I said gravely. "I found a house that I think might be yours. Can you take a look at this picture on my phone and tell me if it's where you live?"

Obediently, the chihuahua trotted over to where I stood. I knelt to show the image of the white house with the gray trim to her, shielding my phone's screen with my free hand so the sun wouldn't glare down on the glass.

"It sort of looks like my house," Lexi said. "But I can't smell it, so I don't know for sure."

Right. I should have realized that Lexi, like all dogs, relied on her nose for identifying objects and places, not her eyes.

Since my camera hadn't come equipped with Smell-o-Vision, though, this was about the best I could do.

"Well, look at the shapes of the trees and the way the front path winds," I told her, doing my best to keep the disappointment out of my voice. "When Milton took you for a walk, you'd go up that path to get to the front door, wouldn't you?"

Lexi stared back at the phone, her sandy brown eyebrows drawing together. The image was so comical, it looked like it should be a meme or something, even though I knew the situation was serious enough.

"Maaayyyybe," she responded at last, drawing out the syllables as she continued to stare at the phone. "I just don't know. But I think those pointy flowers blooming by the path look familiar."

"Irises," I supplied, and told myself it was good to have another data point. Again, irises were pretty common in this part of the world, but not every house had them planted out front, and the image I was showing her now had a fairly impressive bed of them flanking the walk that led to the front door.

Lexi's tail made a half-hearted wag. "Then maybe that's my house?"

The sentence ended on an upward inflection, letting me know she still wasn't sure but, like most dogs, was doing her best to make a human happy.

It wasn't the best clue in the world. Lacking anything else, however, I thought I'd still have to pursue it and see where it led.

Even if it turned out to be a dead end.

Chapter 3

Surreal Estate

The dogs remained outside while I went into the secondary bedroom I used as an office so I could open up my laptop and do some research. I wasn't feeling very hopeful about the situation, but since I couldn't think of anything better to do, I figured I might as well make the attempt.

However, I'd barely entered my password before my phone rang.

A quick glance at the screen told me it was Noah calling, and I couldn't help smiling when I saw his number displayed there.

"How's it going with our little stray?" he asked.

"Fine," I said. "She's getting along great with Milo." I paused there for a moment, glad I'd maintained enough presence of mind to keep myself from saying Lexi's name, because of course Noah would want to know how I'd figured that out when the little dog had been found without a collar or any other form of identification.

And I absolutely couldn't mention that I now knew Lexi lived in a big white house with gray trim because I'd seen it in my scrying mirror.

Yep, that would go over real well.

"That's good," Noah said, then went on, "Courtney took some pictures of the dog and posted them on the local lost pets groups on Facebook and Nextdoor, but so far, no one seems to have recognized her or have any idea where she might have come from."

"I don't think she's from Salem," I replied, and got a puzzled silence on the other end of the line.

Then Noah asked, "What makes you think that?"

Well, at least that question was easy enough to answer without bringing up the fraught topic of my magic. "She keeps sniffing the air and looking out toward the shoreline, which tells me she doesn't really know much about the ocean. That's why I get the feeling she must live inland somewhere and got dumped here for whatever reason."

"It's strange that someone would do that," Noah said. "I mean, I hate to put this kind of spin on things, but she's a valuable dog. I can see someone stealing her to try selling her on the black market, but why would they dump her at the park if they were trying to make some money off her?"

I hadn't even thought about the situation in that light. The relative worth of a purebred animal had never entered my mind, since I took each dog who came into my life as an individual, not as what a particular breed could fetch...pardon the expression...on the canine black market.

If someone hadn't cast a spell on Lexi to make her speak, I might have dismissed all this as petty theft and nothing more. But someone had taken her from her home for a reason, and I had to figure out why.

"I have no idea," I said. "None of this seems to make very much sense."

Well, at least that comment was true.

"We'll keep looking," he assured me. "But thanks again for watching her in the meantime. I know other fosters in the area who could have taken her in, but your house seemed like the best place for her to be."

My heart warmed at those words, although I told myself Noah might have said them simply because he knew I only had Milo with me right now and not any other foster animals who might have taken up too much of my attention.

"It's fine," I said. "She's a sweet dog, and, like I said, she and Milo seem to get along really well together." I paused, then decided I should go ahead and ask. "Are you still coming over tonight?"

"Sure," he replied at once, without a single bit of hesitation. "It'll be good for me to check on the dog."

"That's the only reason?" I inquired, my tone arch.

Again, his response was immediate. "You know it isn't. But it'll be good for me to see her with Milo. Six-thirty? I can bring the pizza."

I'd been planning to call in the order myself, but if Noah wanted to pick it up on his way over here, that would work out even better. I had no idea whether Lexi was as much of a fiend for table scraps as Milo, but I figured I'd find out soon enough.

"Great," I said. "Then I'll see you at six-thirty."

"See you then."

We ended the call there, and I set my phone back down on the desk before reaching for the connector so I could hook it up to my laptop. I could have done this all on the phone, I supposed, but since I needed to look at pictures of houses in detail, squinting at its tiny screen didn't seem like a very good idea.

Soon enough, I had the images I'd captured from the scrying mirror downloaded to my computer. I chose the clearest one and headed over to Google, then uploaded it to the search engine.

At once, it brought up a series of images that, at first glance, looked very much like the house from the mirror. However, as I studied each of them in turn, I could tell they weren't the right place—this one had roses instead of irises planted along the front walk, or the trim on another one was soft blue instead of gray. I told myself not to get discouraged and kept going, looking at image after image of big white houses until my brain started to feel like it could never imagine a home being painted any other color.

But then....

That was the house. Or at least, if it wasn't, it must have been built by the same company and landscaped by the same person, because it looked identical. I clicked on the image, and it took me to an old real estate listing, one that showed the house as being off-market but which still gave me an address.

92 Highland Street, Dunstable, Massachusetts.

The place had been off-market for nearly five years, which told me Lexi had probably lived there her entire lifetime. And whoever this "Milton" was, obviously he did well for himself, since even five years ago before real estate prices had gone utterly insane, the house had sold for well over a million dollars.

Dunstable was about forty miles inland, which explained why the dog didn't seem too familiar with the ocean. True, it wasn't exactly the world's most strenuous drive or anything close to it, but I knew a lot of people seemed to stick close to home and didn't seem too inclined to take day trips, meaning she might never have been to the coast before being dumped in Salem.

At any rate, I now had an address, which meant I needed to drive over there and see if I could talk to this Milton person. No doubt he must be missing his dog very much, but Dunstable was just far enough out of Salem's orbit that he probably wouldn't have seen any of the posts on Nextdoor or Facebook...assuming, of course, that he even spent time on social media. Lots of people didn't, after all.

Problem was, I had the dogs to worry about. If it was just Milo, I knew I could leave him at home without any problem. However, since I didn't know who had cast that spell on Lexi or why she'd been dumped at a park forty miles from where she lived, I didn't feel comfortable leaving her at home unguarded.

Well, there's no reason why you should leave her here at all, I told myself. *If you're going to her house, then you should take her along so you can reunite her with her owner.*

That plan made sense. Also, even though the spell was still in place and didn't seem to show any sign of wearing off any time soon, it appeared the enchantment wouldn't allow Lexi to talk to ordinary human beings, which meant it should be safe to leave her at her house with Milton.

Well, except for the part where she'd already been dognapped once. Did I really want to take that risk again?

Damn it.

I reasoned with myself that Lexi's owner would be doubly careful from now on and wouldn't let her out of his sight, but I couldn't know that for sure. Also, this wasn't about keeping her away from ordinary dog snatchers. The dark-haired witch I'd seen in the scrying mirror had cast that spell on the little chihuahua for a reason, even if I hadn't been able to figure out why. Who was to say she wouldn't go after the dog a second time? Witches were far from omnipotent, but they definitely had an advantage over regular people who couldn't use magic, which meant Lexi's owner wouldn't be able to do much to protect himself from a user of magic if they were determined to get the dog away from him.

Double damn it.

I wrestled with myself for a few minutes, then decided to compromise by bringing both dogs along but making sure my Land Rover was guarded by every protection spell I could think of. Milo had great protective instincts anyway, and if I told him he needed to keep watch on Lexi while I went to talk to the little dog's owner, he'd guard her with his life.

Luckily, Dunstable was less than an hour away, so I had plenty of time to drive there and back and be home long before Noah planned to show up with some pizza. I supposed it showed how well we'd gotten to know each other over the past few months that he hadn't even asked what kind I wanted, but had remembered I liked everything on it except anchovies. Maybe I lived near the coast, but that didn't mean I wanted those nasty little fishies on my pizza.

Now that I had a plan, I left the office and headed out into the backyard, where the two dogs were lying on that same patch of grass, clearly intent on soaking up every ray of sun they possibly could. It felt a little mean to disturb them, but because I hoped this foray would end with Lexi back in her owner's hands, I knew we needed to get going.

"Hey, there," I called out cheerfully. "Time to go on a road trip."

Milo was such a good dog that he gave up his beloved front seat so Lexi could ride shotgun. She stood on her two tiny hind legs and gazed out the window as the landscape passed by, clearly enjoying herself.

"Do you recognize any of this countryside?" I asked once we were out of Salem and cruising along I-95.

Lexi didn't turn away from the window, although I thought I saw her head tilt slightly as she considered my question. "Maybe?" she said. "What is that big place coming up on the right?"

"The Burlington Mall," I supplied, even as I got over one lane so I'd be ready to make the transition to Highway 3. "Did Milton ever bring you here?"

"I think he left me in the parking lot a couple of times while he went inside," she responded. Then her little nose wrinkled as she added, "It wasn't very much fun."

No, I supposed it wouldn't be. But because she looked very well groomed and obviously cared for, I had to believe Milton had only left her in the car those times when the weather would have cooperated, when it wasn't too hot or too cold. Also, even though I'd only been there once or twice, I thought I remembered there was a kind of high-end pet shop in the mall, the sort of place where he might have bought the pretty red collar she was wearing, obviously real leather and not something that looked like he could have gotten it at a chain store.

If Lexi had been here, though, it meant we were on the right track by going to Dunstable...or at least, I hoped we were. The mall was located at almost the halfway point on our trip and wouldn't have been too much of a drive for the mysterious Milton.

I reached over and gave Lexi's soft little ears a quick ruffle, hoping the caress would reassure her. She didn't seem quite as affectionate as Milo, but I couldn't say for sure whether that was because of the difference in their breeds or a simple matter of personality.

Or she could have been anxious because she had no idea what had happened to her, which was completely understandable.

The three of us were quiet as I drove the rest of the way to Dunstable, where I got off the highway and onto Main Street, following it as it looped its way along lovely tree-lined roads and passed a cafe and what looked like the local bar. Soon enough, though, I saw Highland Street coming up on the right and turned.

This neighborhood looked almost exactly the way I'd pictured it, with large houses—white, naturally—set back on expansive grounds, some with more trees clustered around, others with wide green lawns that were just starting to turn yellow as fall began to set in. Now I could see Lexi's tail wagging, and I smiled.

"You know this street?"

Her tail wagged a little harder. "Yes. This is my street!"

The happiness in her voice was clear enough… as if I couldn't already tell how glad she was to be back in familiar surroundings, thanks to the way her feathery tail was going back and forth at practically light speed.

And there was number nine-two, at the very end of the road. As I'd seen in the scrying mirror, it was a large white house with pale gray trim and shutters. The exuberant irises from my vision were long gone, of course, but I still recognized the sword-shaped leaves of the plants bordering the front walk and guessed they would be absolutely spectacular in April and May.

No sign of life, but I told myself not to worry about that. After all, the house had a garage around to one side, and I guessed Milton must have his car parked in there. This definitely wasn't the kind of neighborhood where people left their vehicles at the curb or in the driveway. No, everything was perfect enough for a postcard.

Or a real estate listing.

Lexi's tail was wagging so quickly that I wondered if she was about to take flight. However, I wasn't about to let her go into the house with me right away. No, I'd already decided it would be better for me to get the lay of the land before I brought her inside.

"Okay, you two," I said, twisting in my seat so I could get a look at Milo as well. He sat upright, brown eyes clear and focused, which telegraphed that he already knew I planned to have the dogs stay behind while I went up to the front door. "I'm going to see if Milton's home. If he's not, we can try circling back to that café we passed on the way in. It looked like they have a patio where we could sit for a while until he comes home from work."

Which would be a pretty long wait, considering it was now just a little past three o'clock. Still, I thought I'd be able to make it home in time to meet Noah even if we had to cool our heels here until four-thirty or five. Maybe I'd be cutting it a little close, but since all I had to do was wait for him to show up with the pizza, it wasn't as if I had to rush home to start making an elaborate meal.

However, neither of the dogs seemed too worried about any snags in my plan, although Lexi said, "Why can't I go to the door with you? It's my house—I can smell it."

Well, that was something. Still, even though we'd come to the right place, I wasn't about to take any more risks than I absolutely had to.

"No, you should wait in the car with Milo," I told her. "We still don't know who cast that spell on you or whether it was the same person who dropped you in the park, so better to have you stay in here where it's safe until I know for sure it's okay to bring you inside."

Lexi's pert ears drooped a little at my warning, but I noticed how she didn't try to argue with me and instead abandoned her post on the front seat so she could go sit in back with Milo. "Okay," she said. "I'll wait here."

With that settled, I gave both the dogs what I hoped was an encouraging smile before climbing out of the driver's seat, hoisting my purse over my shoulder, and locking the car behind me. I'd already cracked the windows, and since it was a mild day with temperatures not much more than sixty-five, I knew they'd be fine as long as this didn't take too long.

A quick pause to lay another protection spell on the vehicle—just to be safe—and then I began to make my way up the long front walk. As I went, I looked from side to side, trying to see if I could detect anything out of the ordinary, but everything here looked tidy and peaceful. Sure, there were a few fallen leaves on the wide front lawn, and yet I couldn't find anything too strange about that. We were coming up on that time of year, after all, and even the most dedicated gardener in the world wouldn't be able to keep up with leaf fall in New England once it really got going.

The front door of the house was painted deep green, a nice contrast to the overall white and gray color scheme. I pressed the doorbell button and heard an answering *ding-dong* deep within the house, so I settled in to wait.

And wait...and wait. The seconds ticked past, and I frowned. Obviously, the doorbell worked, or I wouldn't have heard it respond to my push on the button. Still, maybe Milton was up on the second floor, and for whatever reason, the bell wasn't as audible up there.

Easy enough to fix.

I raised my hand and knocked, two smart raps that I hoped were confident without sounding intrusive. Once again I waited, although I glanced away from the door long enough to see that my Land Rover—looking shabbier than ever in this upscale neighborhood—still waited peacefully at the curb, the two dogs inside just a couple of blurs past the lightly tinted glass.

When I looked back at the front door, it hadn't budged. Clearly, Milton wasn't at home.

Or maybe he was, and didn't want to come to the door because he thought I was a solicitor or something.

"Milton?" I called out, feeling vaguely foolish. However, since I'd driven all this way, it would be even more stupid to turn around and leave without exhausting all the possibilities. For all I knew, he was standing right inside the door and listening, in which case, I needed to let him know exactly what was going on. "My name's Charity Hughes. I'm from Salem—I found your dog."

All right, that was a slight oversimplification of the truth, but I thought it better to be as brief as possible.

Still no answer. I frowned, knowing I'd pretty much exhausted the socially accepted ways of dealing with this kind of situation...and trying to determine whether I needed to attempt some not-so-socially acceptable ones.

Another glance over my shoulder, only this time to make sure no suspicious neighbor had decided to come out and water their lawn and keep an eye on the redhead in the black shirt and jeans at the same time. However, everything still looked as calm and peaceful as a movie set, leading me to believe the residents of this street must all be off at whatever jobs they held in order to be able to afford these impressive houses.

The nice thing about door-unlocking spells was that they didn't leave any evidence behind to show that a lock had been meddled with. No, there was always the plausible deniability that the door hadn't quite caught or the tumblers had failed, and if it turned out Milton was indeed skulking around inside, I'd just tell him I'd knocked and rung the bell, and had only come inside when I realized the front door was unlocked.

Technically, that was still trespassing, but I figured I'd take the risk.

I laid my hand on the fancy brass latch and murmured the words of the spell under my breath.

Whispered words, soft and clear,
Unlock this door so I may enter here.

At once, the green-painted door swung inward. I didn't go inside immediately, but instead stood on the threshold and peered into the home's interior. It was dark in there, the curtains in the rooms to either side of the central hallway pulled shut, and yet I could still see the same floor of shining dark wood that I'd glimpsed in that vision of the witch casting her spell on Lexi. An expensive Persian runner stretched the entire length of the corridor.

"Milton?" I ventured again.

Only silence, which was about what I'd expected. Another glance over my shoulder to reassure myself that my SUV was still fine and none of the neighbors had come out to peer at the stranger on Milton's doorstep, and then I went inside and quietly closed the door behind me.

It was chilly in there, cold and dark after the bright, mild day outside. I found myself shivering, which was silly, since I knew the temperature difference could only have been a couple of degrees.

Or maybe it wasn't the temperature, but some sensation of wrongness that seemed to beat against my temples. I couldn't even exactly say why; I wasn't a psychic, wasn't the kind of witch who could pick up on vibrations or anything like that. Somehow, though, my lizard brain was telling me this was a place I really didn't want to be.

However, I made myself keep going after a quick glance into the living and dining rooms, both of which had been impeccably furnished with antiques that I guessed were real and not reproductions, and both of which were completely devoid of human life.

Straight ahead was the family room, and off to one side a large kitchen that looked as though it had been recently remodeled, with white quartz countertops and a white subway tile backsplash that contrasted nicely with the dark cabinetry. However, my brain didn't have a chance to record much more than that single impression, because my gaze inevitably went to the one thing out of place in that almost impossibly neat space.

A man's body, lying with one arm stretched toward the French doors that opened on the backyard.

Chapter 4

A Body Meet a Body

"And how do you know Milton Keyes?" the police chief asked. Dunstable was so tiny that, while it had its own police force, it definitely didn't have a dedicated homicide division. The woman who'd taken my call must have decided a murder was unusual enough in their quiet community that it required the department head to handle things. Chief Bill Stanton looked like he was around fifty, with close-cropped graying hair and sharp blue eyes, and didn't seem like the sort of person who had much use for witches and magic.

Not that I intended to bring up any of those topics.

I blinked. "I don't know Milton," I replied. "I mean, I rescued his dog yesterday and was bringing her back to him when I found...."

The words trailed off—not that Chief Stanton needed me to finish the sentence. "When you found his body," he said crisply. "And how were you able to get into the house?"

Luckily, I'd already anticipated his question. "The door was unlocked," I replied. "Maybe the person who killed him unlocked it?"

The chief's mouth thinned. "We have someone looking into that." He paused, narrowed sky-blue eyes studying me for a moment, while all I could do was stand there and hope I didn't look too much like a burglar. No, I wasn't particularly dressed up, but at least I had on a real blouse and flats, and not the T-shirt and tennis shoes combo I tended to wear on my days off when the weather allowed. "Want to tell me why you thought it was a good idea to just walk into the house, even if the door wasn't locked?"

Right now, it wasn't sounding like a good idea at all. At least I'd retained the presence of mind to keep my lip zipped about Lexi being in my car only a few hundred feet from the spot where the police chief and I currently stood, and it didn't seem as though either of the deputies collecting evidence inside the house had thought to peer into the Land Rover to see if anyone else was in there.

"I guess I wasn't really thinking," I said, assuming a lopsided smile that I hoped Chief Stanton would consider charming. Judging by the way his lips thinned, I had to believe my gambit hadn't been terribly successful. "I rang the doorbell and knocked on the door, and then I just sort of put my hand on the latch and realized the door wasn't locked. I called inside, thinking maybe Mr. Keyes had forgotten to lock it the last time he'd gone out front, but when he didn't answer, I went inside to see what was going on."

Obviously, I hadn't had any idea what Milton's last name was when I embarked on this little adventure, but the police chief had let it slip while he was talking to me, and it seemed smart to act as though I'd known it all along.

"And that was when you found his body."

I nodded, my throat tightening a little. No, I had never seen the man before today and definitely didn't have any personal ties to him, and yet it was awful to find someone like that, to know from the second you caught sight of them that something terrible must have happened.

"He wasn't moving," I said. "I called his name again, but I could tell he was dead. That's when I called 9-1-1."

Some part of me had thought that was a foolish thing to do, that it would have been better to back out quietly, close the door behind me, and magically remove any fingerprints I might have left behind, but I'd dismissed the thought almost right away. No matter what kind of trouble this current intrusion got me into, I couldn't have left the man lying there like that when he might not have been discovered for days...or even longer.

To my relief, Chief Stanton didn't ask me how I knew Milton Keyes was dead. Then again, you didn't have to be a forensics expert to see the massive pool of blood that had formed beneath him, blood that had apparently flowed from a stab wound in his chest, although I hadn't gotten close enough to determine the extent of the damage. He'd been lying on his side, crumpled as if he'd fallen there with that one arm reaching out toward the French doors. Had his killer fled the scene by that route?

Well, if the murderer had left any fingerprints behind, I had no doubt the police chief's deputies would find them. They'd spent a long time on that door before moving on to the countertops in the kitchen. In fact, they were still working there now as Chief Stanton and I held our tense little convo.

The chief made another note on his yellow pad, but then, to my infinite relief, he tucked it and his pen away in an interior pocket of his jacket. "Thank you for your cooperation, Ms. Hughes. I or someone else from my department will be in touch if we need anything else."

I nodded, but, even though I wanted nothing more than to flee the scene, I knew my story would sound hollow to him if I didn't ask the question.

"What should I do about Mr. Keyes' dog?"

An expression of impatience passed over Chief Stanton's sharp features, as though he thought the dog's fate should be pretty low on his list of priorities right then. However, he sounded mild enough as he said, "We can locate a foster home for the dog nearby if you don't want to keep watching her. However, if you don't mind having her for a while longer, at least until we can contact Mr. Keyes' next of kin, that would be a help."

"I can do that," I said quickly. "You have my phone number, so just let me know whenever you need me to bring her back here."

"I appreciate that, Ms. Hughes."

Since it was clear he wanted me out of the way so he could confer with his deputies, I didn't say anything else, only gave a brief bob of my head before I hurried out the door to the car. Once there, I quickly unlocked it, got into the driver's seat, and fastened my seatbelt.

"What happened?" Lexi asked. As soon as I'd gotten into the Land Rover, she'd jumped back into the passenger seat and was now staring at me with imploring dark eyes. "You were in there forever, and then all those other cars drove up."

"I'm sorry it took so long," I told her, even as my heart ached over what I knew I needed to say to her. However, I waited until I'd pulled away from the curb and was safely away from the house before

I allowed myself to continue. "And Lexi...I'm so, so sorry, but it seems as though Milton has been killed."

Honestly, there wasn't much "seem" about the situation—the man had been obviously, irrevocably dead—but I thought I needed to soft-pedal the horrible truth somehow.

Her oversized ears, just as feathery as her tail, immediately flattened. "He *what?*"

Now I wished I had waited until we'd gotten home to tell her, just because I was now driving through unfamiliar territory and couldn't exactly reach over to take her in my arms.

As usual, Milo came to the rescue, squeezing himself between the two front seats so he could use the center console to sort of launch himself next to Lexi on the passenger seat, where he immediately nuzzled his head against her. "It's okay," he said in consoling tones. "Charity took me in after my mistress was murdered, and I'm sure she'll take you in, too."

Oops. Not that I wasn't willing to give Lexi as much time as she needed to recover from her master's death, but I knew I couldn't take in every animal who lost their owner. For one thing, I didn't have the space, and for another, I had no idea how long the spell of speech that unknown witch had cast on the chihuahua would even last. Would Milo be feeling quite so generous if it turned out he wouldn't have someone he could talk to during the long hours I was working at the store?

Well, knowing Milo, he probably would. Not for the first time, I had to wonder how a witch like Darla Fitzgerald could have raised such a kind and loving animal.

Lexi didn't look terribly consoled. "Charity's house isn't very big," she sniffed.

No, compared to Milton Keyes' oversized home, my place, which was barely 1,800 square feet, probably felt like a shoebox. However, Lexi had just had a terrible shock and definitely wasn't trying to edit anything she said, so I wasn't going to indulge the flicker of annoyance that went through me following her words.

"There's room," I said, and left it at that. "And we don't have to make any permanent decisions now. I think it's better if we all just take this one day at a time for the moment and wait to see how everything turns out."

Lexi gave a shake, which I thought might have been her way of replying. Milo moved a bit closer to her, and then she lay down as he cuddled up next to the little dog. Once they were settled, he sent me a sideways glance, as if to tell me he'd take care of her for now.

And thank God for that. I could tell my hands wanted to shake as well, except they were wrapped firmly around the steering wheel. No, it wasn't as if I'd known Milton Keyes, but still, being that close to someone who'd died violently was an awful shock to the system no matter how many times I might have witnessed it before.

All I could do now was get us all safely back to Salem...and then try to figure out what in the world I was supposed to do next.

The drive home passed without incident, though, and I pulled into the driveway at a little past four. No thought of trying to do anything useful, like I might have if we hadn't all been dealing with the tragedy of Milton's death.

Instead, the three of us went into the living room, where I asked Lexi if she wanted me to turn on the TV or maybe some music. Listlessly, she replied, "TV, please," so I picked up the remote and turned on *Animal Planet,* since that was a favorite of Milo's and of the other familiars who'd stayed with me in the past.

That seemed to be fine with Lexi; she curled up in my lap and seemed content to stay there as I gently stroked her soft silky fur, while Milo took his place at the foot of my oversized couch. After a while, I could tell she'd fallen asleep, which was probably the best thing for her. However, I didn't move or stop petting her, doing my best to tell her she was safe here and that she could be a part of our little family for as long as necessary.

Would it be forever? I had no idea, since I knew absolutely nothing about Milton Keyes except his address and his name. I didn't know if he'd been married—doubtful, or I assumed Lexi would have mentioned a wife by now—or if he had family members who might want to take in his orphaned dog. Yes, she was an adorable little thing and I had no doubt plenty of families would be more than happy to adopt her, but I wasn't going to let myself think about that until I had some more answers.

The room got darker as the hour moved past six, the time when I normally would have gone around the house and closed the drapes and turned on a few lights. Because Lexi still slept, though, I didn't want to move, telling myself the glow from the TV would be enough to provide some illumination.

And then we all jumped as the doorbell rang.

"That's my boyfriend, Noah," I told Lexi, giving her a couple of reassuring pats. "He's bringing over pizza."

For the first time since we'd gotten the awful news about her master, she looked a little less woebegone. "Pizza"? she asked hopefully.

"Yes, pizza," I replied, glad she was able to show interest in food, if nothing else. "With pepperoni and sausage and all kinds of good stuff. But now I need to answer the door."

Gently, I set her on the floor and then hurried over to let Noah in. A while back, we'd given each other keys to our respective houses, but we still liked to knock when we visited, viewing the keys more for emergency access than anything else.

He came in, pizza box in hand, then took one look at my face and said, "What happened?"

"I'll tell you in a minute," I replied, even as I realized that, since I'd been sitting on the couch with Lexi this whole time, I hadn't had a chance to set the table and get out a bottle of wine the way I normally would have when Noah was bringing over takeout. "Let me just get the table settled."

Still looking concerned, he nodded and went over to the table to set down the pizza, while I hurriedly switched on some lights, then got out placemats and paper napkins and a red blend I'd had sitting in the wine rack on the kitchen counter. If I'd been thinking straight, I might have grabbed the chianti I'd bought a week ago rather than the blend, but right then I was more concerned about getting us sitting down than worrying about wine pairings.

During all this, Lexi and Milo waited off to the side, both of them appearing to realize they needed to stay out from underfoot lest they delay the meal that much longer. Soon enough, Noah and I had seated ourselves, and he'd reached for the bottle of wine to open it—not that it needed expert intervention, since it had a screw cap and not a regular cork.

After we'd both sipped the wine...and realized it was a lot better than the screw cap might have indicated...Noah said, "You look like you've had a shock. Is everything okay?"

No, everything was not okay. "I was able to find out where Lexi lives," I said, and Noah raised an eyebrow.

"'Lexi'?" he repeated.

"Yes," I said. I knew I'd have to tell him a pack of lies to cover up the magic that had led me to the house on Highland Street, so I took a breath and launched into the story I'd made up on the drive back from Dunstable. "I knew you had Courtney checking on Nextdoor and Facebook to see if anyone had posted about the missing dog, but I thought I'd go ahead and just do a general Google search and see what I could find. Lexi was listed on a lost and missing chihuahuas website, along with her owner's information. I tried to call, but there wasn't any answer, so I figured the best thing to do was just take her home."

"You drove over to Dunstable this afternoon?" Noah asked, expression startled.

"It's not even an hour away," I reminded him.

"True, but...." A lift of the shoulders, and

then he seemed to remember that we should be dishing up pizza, because he reached inside the box and snagged a piece for me and then one for himself.

The two dogs had already positioned themselves in the spot between Noah's place at the head of the table and where I sat to his right, and as soon as they saw the pizza hit our plates, their tails started wagging.

Normally, I would have allowed myself a bite or two before I started giving scraps to the dogs, but this was anything but a normal day. I pulled a piece of pepperoni off my slice, broke it in half, and then gave a section to Lexi and the other to Milo. She looked immediately cheered by this, and I wondered if Milton fed her from the table or whether he had been strict about that sort of thing. Considering her purebred status and the way she appeared to have been very well taken care of, I guessed it was the latter.

Well, I wasn't strict, and she definitely deserved a little happiness in her life right now.

"Anyway," I went on, "I got to her owner's house and found the door unlocked. Noah, someone murdered him."

Clearly, my boyfriend hadn't been expecting that end to the story, because he sat up straighter in his chair, blue eyes widening in shock. "*What?*"

"It looked like he was stabbed, but I didn't get

close enough to tell for sure," I said. "I called the police."

He was shaking his head. "This is crazy."

You don't know the half of it, I thought. I still had absolutely no idea why Milton had been murdered, or why that dark-haired witch had cast that spell of speaking on Lexi. Right now, the whole scenario felt like a puzzle that had been dropped on the floor and had about half its pieces missing.

"I know," I said, and finally took a bite of pizza. It had cooled down a little but still tasted wonderful, reminding me that it had been hours and hours since I'd last eaten. "The police didn't have a lot to say, but I assume they'll contact me if they need any more information. Oh, and Chief Stanton told me to keep Lexi for now until they can figure out if there's any next of kin who might want her."

"Poor dog," Noah responded, and tugged a piece of sausage loose from his pizza so he could lean down and give it to her.

Her flag of a tail waved in joy, telling me Lexi appreciated the attention. As excited as she was about the treat, though, she was still gentle as she took it from his fingers, not biting at all the way some dogs did when they got too wrapped up in the moment.

"You do seem to get the ones who've lost their owners to tragedy," Noah went on, his tone musing as he looked down at Lexi and Milo—who'd also gotten a bite of sausage so he wouldn't feel left out. "It's good that she and Milo seem to get along so well."

"There could be a family member who wants her," I replied. While I was definitely glad that the two dogs seemed to have already bonded, I didn't want to get too attached, not when everything was so up in the air. "It's really early in the investigation, so I'm not sure what's going to happen."

Noah acknowledged my comment with a slight incline of his head, then sipped some of his wine. I could tell from his expression that he thought I was going to end up with Lexi as a permanent part of my menagerie.

Maybe I would, but I knew it was far too soon to be making those kinds of plans. About all I could do now was try to give her a safe, happy place to stay until we heard whether she had some family who were willing to give her a home.

"Did it look like there was a struggle?" Noah asked after setting down his wine glass so he could reach for his pizza.

"Not that I could tell," I said. "The house was beautiful, immaculate. It hardly looked as if anyone even lived there. The only thing out of place was...."

I didn't bother to finish the sentence, but the grim nod Noah gave as my words trailed off told me he'd gotten my meaning all too well. We ate in silence for a few minutes then, neither of us wanting to speculate too much with Lexi sitting right there and eyeing every morsel that went into our mouths. True, Noah could have no idea she understood what we were saying and had probably decided to let it go purely out of deference to the uncomfortable subject matter.

A few minutes later, though, he said, "Are you going to take her to work with you tomorrow?"

Good question. I hadn't really thought that far ahead, but since the store was open Tuesdays through Saturdays, I didn't have a lot of time to figure out what I should do with my latest canine charge.

"I'm not sure yet," I said. "Under normal circumstances, I would've said she'd be fine staying here with Milo, since they have the dog door and I know he'd look out for her. But with the way her master was killed and she was dumped at that park...."

Once again, I let the words trail off, since I honestly didn't know what I should say next. Noah wiped his fingers on a napkin, then reached over and laid his hand on mine.

"It's a lot," he replied. "Maybe you should have Sage cover for you for the day. You haven't asked her to do that for a while."

True, it had been months since I'd needed my

assistant to watch the store for me while I dealt with whatever murder that had been dropped in my lap that week. All the same, I didn't want her to think I needed her to bail me out whenever things got too crazy.

On the other hand, Lexi had just suffered a terrible shock. Even though it might have been all right for her to come with me to the shop, I'd be taking her to yet another place she didn't know—and one that could sometimes be kind of hectic, although I had to admit that Tuesdays in mid-September weren't generally my busiest times.

And that was why it would probably be okay to stay home. Making Sage work solo on a Friday or Saturday was one thing, but asking her to cover for me on a sleepy weekday should be all right.

"I'll text her," I told Noah, and something in his expression relaxed. He couldn't know everything that had been going on, obviously, but he loved animals and clearly thought it would be much better for Lexi if I gave her at least another day where I would be around the whole time and she could try to get more acclimated to her surroundings.

"I'm glad," he said simply.

With the matter resolved—well, unless Sage told me she had a last-minute doctor's appointment or some other reason why I couldn't leave her alone at the store—Noah and I went back to our meals, giving the two dogs some more little scraps along the way. And after we were done, we all went back into the living room to watch some more TV, with Lexi climbing onto his lap almost as soon as he settled himself on the couch. Our eyes met as Milo snuggled in between Noah and me, and even though it was dim enough in there, with only the TV and a single table lamp for illumination, I could see the way his mouth curved in the faintest of smiles and I knew he felt it, too.

Somehow...somehow, this felt right.

Chapter 5

The Heart of the Matter

Noah didn't stay the night, however, because we both guessed Lexi would want to snuggle with Milo and me, and any extracurricular activities would definitely be off the table. Instead, he kissed me good night, told me he'd see if he could take a break in the middle of the day so he could bring over some sandwiches, and headed out to the driveway where his pickup truck was parked.

I told myself it was fine. In a way, this felt almost more fun, because we rarely got to see each other during work hours, as he was busy at his vet clinic and I generally didn't take a lot of time off, sabbaticals here and there for murder investigations notwithstanding. But since I'd exchanged texts with Sage the night before and knew she was fine with holding down the fort at Full Moon Apothecary, that meant the two dogs and I could have a relaxing day.

Well, mostly relaxing. Chief Stanton had made it sound as though he didn't have any further need of me, but that didn't mean I didn't plan to mount my own investigation based on publicly available information. The only person I knew in law enforcement was Derek Falco, a homicide detective with the Salem police department, and since our interactions were a little fraught thanks to the way he'd asked me out several times and still seemed to be interested despite my relationship with Noah, I didn't think it would be a good idea to ask him to help me out with this one.

After I'd had breakfast—and fed the dogs little bits of my scrambled eggs while I read the online version of the *Salem News*—I went upstairs, showered, and then let them out in the backyard. The air was a little cooler today, the wind from the ocean a bit brisker, but it was still sunny and bright, perfect for Milo and Lexi to play in the grass and then find a sunny spot for a good post-romp nap.

Knowing they should be occupied for a while, I went back to my laptop, a cup of green tea with ginger on the table next to it, and tried to see what I could discover about the late Mr. Keyes.

The news had already hit the local paper—it had a short article saying that local antiques dealer

Milton Keyes had been found dead in his home, but it didn't offer much more beyond a few short lines stating facts I already knew. But the part about him being an antique dealer explained all the gorgeous furniture I'd spied in his house...and also gave me an idea as to how he might have been able to afford his expensive home in the first place.

A quick search told me he had a store in Dunstable called Once Upon a Time and that he'd owned it for the past fifteen years. A little more digging provided the information that Milton Keyes had been forty-eight years old at the time of his death and didn't appear to have a wife or children. As far as I could tell, he'd lived in that big house with only Lexi for company.

Well, some people didn't like cohabiting with a crowd, so I supposed that part of his background wasn't so strange. A brief mention in the Dunstable *Clarion* showed him celebrating the tenth anniversary of his store opening, with a woman identified as his sister, Adelaide Hanover, standing next to him. I could see the family resemblance, since they were both tall and attractive, with hair a muted gray tone in the photo that I guessed had been medium brown in real life. The man I'd seen lying on the floor of his family room had some silver hairs at his temples, but since the photo was more than five years old, that slight discrepancy didn't seem too unusual.

Had Adelaide Hanover been informed of her brother's death? I had to believe so—as far as I could tell, she seemed to be his only close relative and had probably been his emergency contact.

Since hers was a fairly unusual name, I went ahead and Googled her as well. She was three years younger than her brother and lived in Lowell, and appeared to be divorced and had one child, a daughter who was eleven years old.

Had the girl been close to her uncle?

It was impossible to guess at family dynamics from little snippets gleaned here and there on the internet, so I wouldn't even bother to try. I couldn't help thinking, however, that an eleven-year-old girl might love to have a little dog like Lexi as part of the family.

That thought had only just passed through my mind when Milo and the chihuahua burst through the dog door and headed straight for the water bowls on the other side of the kitchen. Watching them and seeing how natural they were together made me a little sad, though. If Adelaide and her daughter claimed Lexi as theirs, I knew Milo wouldn't be happy...and somehow I guessed Noah wouldn't be, either.

However, I made myself smile at the two dogs as I said, "Did you have fun outside?"

"We did," Lexi replied. "Milo was good at

keeping me busy so I wouldn't have time to be sad."

"He's kind of an expert at that," I told her. "But it's okay to be sad. Losing someone you're close to is hard."

The little dog trotted across the kitchen and stopped where I sat at the kitchen table, then rubbed her head against my leg. I bent down and stroked her soft, feathery ears, thinking how different they felt from Milo's, which were also soft but very heavy. In contrast, Lexi felt like a little wisp of air.

"It is," she agreed. "Being here makes it better, though. Yesterday I wasn't sure whether I would like it, because it's so different from my house. But your yard is more fun."

"I'm glad to hear that," I said, doing my best to keep my mouth from twitching. I had no doubt that Milton Keyes' backyard was far more elegant than mine, but there was a lot to be said for a place where you knew you could roll around in the grass and do pretty much whatever you liked without worrying about messing up your master's pristine landscaping.

Lexi's tail wagged, a gentle swish from side to side. Then she seemed to catch sight of my open laptop and asked, "What are you doing?"

"I'm trying to find out more about your owner," I replied. Since it seemed as if the talking spell was holding for now, I figured it couldn't hurt to ask a few questions...as long as I remembered to be gentle with the little dog and not pry too deeply if a particular subject appeared to be too painful for her. "What can you tell me about him?"

The chihuahua sat back on her haunches, sandy eyebrows pulling together. "I've always lived with him," she replied. "That is, after I left my litter. I was born in a big house on a lot of land not too far from Milton's house, and he brought me home when I was about three months old."

Which was a little young, but not young enough to be considered abusive. Had Lexi been born on a breeding farm, or just in a home where the pet owners hadn't been too careful about spaying their animal?

I suspected it was probably the former, but I decided it was better not to pry.

"He took me everywhere," the little dog went on. "I had a basket in his antique shop, and he'd take me for a walk at lunch and sometimes carried me in a sling if he was going to look for more furniture for his store. He would drive out lots of times to look at tables and chairs and things."

Yes, not everyone loved antiques as much as I did, and I supposed part of the job might involve going to estate sales or maybe just yard sales in search of the perfect Hepplewhite table or Sheraton hutch or whatever other piece he thought would be a good fit for his store. It was sweet that Milton had taken Lexi along on these forays...and also convenient that she was small enough to ride in a sling and therefore couldn't be accused of being in anyone's way.

From what I could tell, he'd been very close to the dog, and it hurt more than ever to think someone had decided to cut his life short in such a terrible way.

"Did he...?"

I had to pause there and think of the best words to use to phrase the question. Unfortunately, there wasn't any good way to ask if a man had terrible enough enemies that they were willing to kill him by stabbing him to death.

"Did he what?" Lexi inquired, tufted ears twitching a little.

"Did Milton have anyone in his life that he wasn't friends with? Someone who might have been angry with him for some reason?"

The chihuahua's head tilted to one side. A few feet away, Milo's gaze was wary, as if he knew why I'd brought up the subject but didn't like my line of questioning very much.

I didn't like it, either, but I had to get to the bottom of this. At the moment, I had no way of knowing if Lexi was safe now that Milton was dead or whether the killer might have an interest in tracking her down, and the only way to find out for sure was to learn who'd driven that knife into his chest. Of course, I hoped the Dunstable police would be able to get to the bottom of his murder on their own without my help, but I couldn't count on that.

"Everyone liked Milton," Lexi informed me. "He was a friendly man who knew everyone. That was also why I liked being his dog—I got to meet new people almost every day. It was never boring."

Well, at least those words reassured me that Lexi wouldn't have a problem hanging out at the store if it turned out she'd become a permanent part of my household.

However, they didn't get me any closer to discovering who might have had a beef with her owner. Generally speaking, you didn't stab someone to death unless you were seriously angry about something.

"You're sure?" I asked. "There wasn't a single person who seemed as if they were upset with him for some reason, who might have had cross words with him?"

Once again, Lexi's head tilted as she considered my question. Maybe the cute little gesture helped her think better. After all, she wasn't a familiar who'd been using language since the time she'd been born. Considering the circumstances, I thought she was doing very well.

"There was that one lady," the dog said, and I

perked right up. A few feet beyond Lexi, Milo also seemed to go alert, his golden-brown eyes intent on the little dog.

"What one lady?" I asked.

"I don't know who she was," Lexi replied. "She didn't smell familiar, so I don't think she was someone who'd been in the store before. But she went up to Milton and asked him what he'd done with the book."

"What did he say?"

Dogs couldn't really shrug, but her shoulders moved in a fairly close approximation of that very human movement. "He told her he wasn't a book dealer, but she was free to look around the shop and see if there was anything among the few he had in stock that she might be interested in. Then she got all angry and told him if it wasn't in the store, he must have it somewhere."

"But he didn't, I assume," Milo put in, and Lexi shook her head.

"No. At least, the store didn't have many books, and it was kind of obvious the one she was looking for wasn't there. She got all puffed out and huffy, and then she left and slammed the door behind her."

What a Karen, was my first thought, but I didn't say the words aloud, as I doubted either dog would get the reference. "What did the lady look like?"

The chihuahua's nose wrinkled, and I got the impression she didn't think a person's looks were what mattered. In the dog world, maybe not, but I couldn't use my nose to track someone down.

"Her hair wasn't like yours...not as bright."

Although dogs weren't completely color blind, they definitely couldn't detect subtle variations in shade and hue. But at least it sounded as if the woman wasn't a redhead, which I supposed narrowed things down a bit.

The teeniest, tiniest bit.

However, it wasn't all about color.

"Was she about the same size as me?"

At least it didn't seem as if Lexi needed to ponder that question for very long. "No, she was taller. Narrow like you, though."

Was that the dog way of saying "slender"?

I supposed I'd take it.

"Was she old or young?"

This time, Lexi didn't seem quite as sure of herself. Her ears went back and she sniffed, as though somehow pulling some extra air through her ultra-sensitive nose would help her to answer my question correctly.

"Not really either," she said after a moment. "Like Milton wasn't exactly young or old."

Middle-aged, then.

All right, so a woman maybe somewhere in her forties or fifties, tall and slim and with brown hair, had gotten in Milton's face about a book she thought he had somewhere in his possession. Why she would believe such a thing, I didn't know, and it sounded to me as though Lexi had already exhausted her memory of the scene.

However, since I didn't have much else to go on, I knew I had to keep trying.

"Did she ever come back to Milton's store?"

This time, the dog's reply was emphatic. "No, she only came in that one time. I was glad about that, because I could tell he wasn't very happy about having her in the shop. She was mean."

I couldn't really argue with that statement... assuming Lexi's account of the encounter was accurate. Then again, dogs didn't lie. They might misrepresent something if their memory of an incident wasn't clear, but it wasn't anything they'd do on purpose.

Still, I couldn't help wondering about the book the woman had been looking for and why it was so important to her. A family heirloom of some kind that had accidentally ended up in one of Milton's antiques hauls?

That sounded like the most likely explanation. Problem was, without access to his records—assuming he even kept accurate accountings of all his purchases and their provenance—I had no idea when or where he might have even acquired such a book.

But he'd claimed not to have it.

I decided to put the incident aside for now, since I didn't have nearly enough information to make an informed judgment about it one way or another. Instead, I asked Lexi, "But there wasn't anyone else except that one woman who might have had a problem with Milton?"

"No," she said promptly.

About what I'd figured, but I'd had to ask.

"Do you know if he was seeing anyone?"

"He saw people every day at the shop."

I reminded myself that dogs could be very literal sometimes, and did my best to rephrase the question. "I meant if he was dating anybody. You know, being in a romantic relationship with someone."

Another head shake, although this one wasn't quite as emphatic. "I don't think so," she said after a pause. "I mean, he was home almost all the time."

"'Almost'?" Milo prompted, speaking for the first time. "So, he went out sometimes?"

Lexi blinked. "He had antiques society meetings to go to a couple of times a month. He told me he couldn't bring me along because dogs weren't allowed in the place where they met."

Hmm. The story could be true...or maybe Milton had been seeing someone, and he'd told Lexi about the antiques society meetings because he hadn't wanted to hurt her feelings. No, it wasn't as though she would have been able to speak back then, but people talked to their dogs all the time—and the dogs probably understood a lot more than their owners thought they did.

Well, checking to see whether there were actually antique society meetings anywhere near Dunstable, Massachusetts, should be easy enough.

"Let me see if I can find out more about those meetings," I told Lexi, and both she and Milo watched in some fascination as I typed in a quick query and then scanned the results. As far as I'd been able to tell from observing Milo's behavior the past couple of months, he regarded anything I did on my laptop as its own form of magic.

Well, I supposed it was a kind of magic, having all the information in the world at my fingertips. Google informed me there was an antique society that met in Boston, but I kind of doubted Milton would have driven that far just to go to a meeting.

Or maybe not. After all, he'd taken Lexi to the Burlington Mall, a drive of almost a half hour. True, Boston was a lot farther away, but....

Then again, when I went to the antique society's website, it informed me they only met once a month, not the several times Milton had told Lexi. So...maybe he had been trying to hide something. Probably not some kind of torrid affair, or he would have disappeared more than just two or three times each month, but maybe he and his unknown girlfriend had liked it that way.

And now I knew I was speculating wildly based on very little evidence. There could have been a perfectly innocent reason why he'd gone off somewhere on a regular basis and left the dog at home. Until I had a lot more facts in hand, I couldn't even begin to guess what might have been going on.

What I really needed were the records from his store, and, even better, access to his phone. Since I doubted the Dunstable police would hand that information over to someone who wasn't in law enforcement, I'd have to come up with some other way of getting a look at Milton's personal effects.

Well, I wasn't entirely without resources. I hadn't quite gotten to the point of desperation where I'd reach out to Derek Falco for help—and I doubted he could even assist me with some of this, since Dunstable was way out of his jurisdiction and I had a feeling Chief Stanton wouldn't be too happy to have a detective from Salem interfering with his investigation—but I could always try the scrying mirror again. Now that Lexi had given me some fairly concrete details, they should help me to focus on that incident at Milton's antique store.

If it had even been significant at all. It could have been a case of someone believing something that wasn't true and lashing out and nothing more.

But I needed to find out for sure.

Chapter 6

Mirror of Her Dreams

Before I got to work on the scrying mirror again, though, I made myself some tea and asked Milo and Lexi whether they'd rather go back outside or head into the living room to relax there. They both said they'd rather lie in the grass for a while, so they promptly headed out the doggy door even as I was refilling my teakettle.

I had no idea if any of this was going to work at all. Scrying didn't come as easily to me as it did some other witches, even if it had performed for me fairly well the last few times I'd tried it.

One good thing was that more than twenty-four hours had passed since I'd last attempted this kind of spell. I'd learned over the years that trying to push it and keep casting a scrying enchantment after I'd already performed it several times in a single day almost always led to failure. But I was fresh now, so to speak, so I figured I'd hope for the best and see what happened.

In the heart of antiques, where history sleeps,
A clash of tempers, secrets it keeps.
Stolen book, echoes in store,
Anger unleashed, artifacts no more.

All right, it didn't sound as if the angry woman had actually destroyed anything in Milton's antique shop, but with spells like this, it was more about evoking the feeling in a scene rather than getting every single little detail right.

Mist gathered in the silver bowl I'd set on the kitchen table and I waited, hoping it would provide me with the sort of crystal-clear image I needed. My phone already sat off to one side, ready to snap a photo if the mirror turned out to reveal something I could actually use.

Then I saw what I guessed was Milton's store, more crowded and cluttered than I would have imagined, considering how tidy his house had been. However, everything in the shop was shiny and dust-free, and what had looked like chaos at first sight definitely wasn't, with everything neatly labeled and easily accessible.

The same man I'd seen in the newspaper photo about the tenth anniversary of the store was standing near the front counter. It was a little jarring to catch a glimpse of him like this and know he was dead...and also to see how alive he seemed, so different from the grainy newspaper photograph, with his warm brown hair and clear gray eyes. Not exactly handsome, but attractive and personable, definitely someone who would have been viewed as quite a catch by any of the unattached women of a certain age in the neighborhood.

Standing a few feet away from him was a woman, tall and slim. Her body was angled away from me so all I could see was the outline of her cheek, but all the same, I couldn't keep myself from letting out a gasp.

The long brown hair caught in a silver clasp... the mid-calf black skirt and accompanying lace-up boots....

It was the woman from the vision I'd seen when I was trying to figure out who'd cast the spell of speech on Lexi.

If only she would turn toward me! The small glimpse I was getting now wouldn't be enough to identify her in a lineup, let alone take a snap with my camera to upload her image to Google.

Milton was frowning, mouth forming a clear enough "no," even though I couldn't hear what he was saying. The woman shook her head and lifted a hand, pointing at him. In fact, she was making little jabbing motions with her index finger, as if to emphasize a point.

Was she casting a spell? I couldn't think of any that required those kinds of hand gestures, but I'd be the first to admit I didn't have every single spell in the world memorized, especially any that involved casting some sort of negative magic.

Also, it would be pretty damn brazen to start throwing spells around in public like that, considering there seemed to be several other customers in the store. I couldn't see much of them except as vague outlines down a different aisle from the one where the hostile witch stood, but I had to believe they must have been embarrassed to witness that kind of scene.

However, nothing seemed to happen to Milton, except that he spread his hands wide, as if to show he couldn't do anything to help her, and seemed to be speaking again. The woman turned and stomped off, moving out of range of the scrying mirror, going so fast there was no hope of my catching her with my phone's camera.

But I'd caught a glimpse of the woman's face as she turned, just enough to make out sharp, half-attractive features and glittering dark eyes. Probably not enough to give an accurate description to a police sketch artist, but possibly enough so that I'd recognize her if I ever bumped into her in person.

I hoped.

For a moment, I contemplated attempting another scrying, but I guessed doing so wouldn't help me very much. As far as the magic was concerned, I'd gotten to see the incident where the strange witch confronted Milton Keyes, and that meant it had done its job. Asking it for a do-over and specifying exact camera angles was the sort of thing that almost invariably ended in failure.

Instead, I reached for my cup of tea, which by that point had cooled down enough so I'd be able to drink it. I sipped the fragrant oolong and stared off toward the kitchen window, which showed me the two dogs, both of them lying in the grass, apparently having a late-morning nap. While I couldn't put aside my worry over who the strange witch was and what she might be planning next, it still made me smile a little to see Lexi and Milo together like that. He was obviously doing whatever he could to make the chihuahua feel comfortable here, and—as far as I could tell, anyway—she seemed to be safe enough. It wasn't as though I had the witchy equivalent of laser-triggered alarms or anything close to that, but at the beginning of every month, I laid down a fresh batch of protection charms on the property, and I supposed they were working as intended.

Still, a determined witch could get past them if she wanted, which led me to believe no one must be actively looking for Lexi. I still didn't know if the strange witch had dumped the dog here in Salem, or if there was yet some other third party involved in the mystery, someone who, for their own obscure reasons, had brought the dog far away from her home territory.

My phone had been silent all morning. My plans with Noah were already set, so I hadn't really expected to hear from him unless he had to cancel our lunch for some reason. However, I'd halfway been hoping I might get a call from Chief Stanton —not because I looked forward to being grilled by him some more, but because I'd thought that even while he was asking me more questions, he might let something slip about the investigation.

Or maybe not. I doubted he had to deal with homicide cases very often, but he still seemed like a pretty tough customer.

Which left me to sit here and wonder what the hell I was supposed to do now.

Look after Lexi, I told myself. *She's all you're really responsible for at the moment.*

True, and yet with an angry witch on the loose who might or might not have killed Milton Keyes but who had definitely put that spell on the dog to make her talk, I didn't feel like it was okay for me to just sit back and work on my knitting.

Not that I knitted, but still.

I finished my cup of tea, then went over to the sink so I could rinse out the mug and put it in the dishwasher. A glance at the clock told me I still had twenty minutes until noon, so I headed outside, thinking I could check on the dogs and maybe look to see if any herbs needed gathering. Almost everything had started to go to seed, but some mustard hung on, along with the rosemary bushes that served as a sort of border between the culinary and medicinal plants.

As soon as I stepped onto the grass, Milo sat up, while next to him, Lexi gave a luxurious stretch. "Is everything okay?" he asked.

"It's fine," I said. No point in mentioning what I'd seen in the mirror, since it hadn't been enough to be truly helpful. "I just thought I'd come gather some herbs while I was waiting for Noah to get here."

Since I'd already told the dogs he would be coming to the house for lunch, my comment didn't get much more than a nod from Milo. Lexi, though, climbed to her feet, eyes shining.

"I like him," she announced.

I'd already gotten that impression, had noticed how the little dog had sort of glommed onto Noah the night before after those initial few moments of wariness. Well, it made sense. I was the one taking care of her right now, but her owner had been a man and it seemed obvious to me that she was more comforted by a male presence.

Smiling, I said, "I like him, too. And I'm pretty

sure he'll give you some bits of his sandwich…if you ask nicely."

"I will," Lexi promised, tail wagging. Then one ear drooped as she added, "I just wish he could hear me talk. Why can't he?"

"Because he's not a witch," I replied, even as I thought I was very, very glad that Noah couldn't understand Lexi's speech. Trying to explain a talking dog would have been a bridge too far. "As far as I can tell, the spell cast on you makes it so only witches can hear what you're saying."

A sniff. "That seems like a silly spell to me."

On the surface, maybe it was. However, I had to wonder if there had been a method to the spell's madness. Could it have been cast that way so whatever information Lexi possessed could only be passed on to a witch?

Of course, that begged the question of the little dog actually having any information that needed to be safeguarded in such a way, and so far, I hadn't seen any indication that she knew anything out of the ordinary.

Maybe it was simply that the enchantment was a difficult one to cast in the first place, and making it so ordinary people could understand the dog added an extra layer of complexity, something the spell caster simply hadn't wanted to deal with. With so many unknowns in the equation, I had a hard time figuring out whether any of it was significant...or whether I was just grasping at straws in order to make sense of the situation.

"I suppose so," I said lightly. "But that's how it seems to be. I'm just glad it's lasting so long, or I might not be able to talk to you, either."

At once, the chihuahua's eyes widened. "You mean it could go away?"

Right then, I wished I'd kept my mouth shut. "I don't think it's going to," I replied hastily. "That is, usually if a spell is going to fade, it would have done so by now. I think it's going to be fine."

Those words seemed to relieve her a little, but I could tell from the worried expression she still wore that she didn't know if she could entirely trust them.

Milo chimed in then, saying, "It's true. If a witch doesn't put a duration on a spell, then it lasts as long as she's alive. Which for most people is a very long time," he added, now with a note of sadness in his voice.

Was he thinking of Darla Fitzgerald, his former mistress, or of Milton Keyes? Both of them had had lives that were cut short, although of course, Milton couldn't have been a witch.

To my relief, Lexi looked somewhat cheered by his words. "It's true. People live much longer than dogs."

Well, unless those dogs were familiars, but I wouldn't bother to point that out. Milo had been raised as a witch's companion and so knew many of the finer details of the magical world, whereas Lexi was new to all this, and both he and I realized it was better not to bombard her with too many details at once.

I was saved from having to reply by the ringing of the doorbell. "Sounds like Noah's here with the sandwiches," I announced, whereupon both dogs scampered for the front door.

As skilled as Milo was at many things, he couldn't open a door, and obviously, Lexi was way too small to reach the knob. They had to wait there, tails wagging, while I followed at a somewhat more sedate pace and opened the door to reveal Noah standing there, a large brown paper bag in one hand.

"Lunch!" he announced cheerfully—and unnecessarily, since I could see he hadn't arrived empty-handed.

"We've been waiting for you," I said, and added with a grin, "In case you hadn't noticed."

He smiled back, and something tight and worried inside me seemed to relax slightly. I might not have been any closer to clearing up this mystery than I'd been the night before when we'd last seen each other, but just having Noah around made me feel worlds better.

"The table's already set," I told him as we headed into the dining room. Nothing fancy, obviously, just plates and placemats and a pitcher of iced tea to go along with our sandwiches, but at least I was a little more prepared than I'd been the night before when he'd arrived with the pizza.

The dogs followed, naturally, all wagging tails and toothy smiles. Noah had already petted both Milo and Lexi as soon as he stepped inside the house, so now we could go ahead and get down to the important stuff—namely, retrieving from the paper bag the sandwiches and the little tub of pasta salad he'd brought along with him.

Marvelous Italian subs for both of us, mine so big that I was pretty sure I'd only be able to eat half of it. Well, that would take care of lunch tomorrow.

"Everyone seems happy and healthy," Noah remarked as he carefully extricated a bit of salami and handed it to Lexi.

"Yes, we're all doing well," I said. "And it's been really quiet, so I think Lexi's going to be safe here."

The sideways look Noah shot me after that comment told me he understood exactly what I was driving at. "Were you worried?"

A very good question. "I was," I replied, then helped myself to a mouthful of salami and soppressata and provolone, all drizzled with oil and vinegar and tart with pepperoncinis. Realizing I was neglecting my own dog, I pulled out a morsel of salami and fed it to him, and his tail thumped happily in response. "Mostly because I still have no idea who left Lexi in that park, and why. It could have been the same person who killed Milton, but that doesn't explain why they would have done something like that in the first place."

Noah inclined his head slightly, but since he was in the middle of taking a bite of sandwich, I had to wait for him to finish chewing before he could respond.

"Have you found out anything more about the murder?"

"Not a lot," I said. "I mean, it made the local paper, but the little article I read online didn't say anything I didn't already know. I did learn that Milton Keyes owned an antique store and he apparently has a sister who lives in Lowell."

That bit of information made Noah's brilliant blue eyes narrow slightly. "Do you think she's going to claim Lexi?"

"I have no idea," I replied. "Chief Stanton knows I have the dog, and I assume he must have passed that information on to Adelaide Hanover, Milton's sister. But I haven't heard anything from her."

"Well," Noah said, "she's had a horrible shock. Maybe she's still trying to deal with what happened to her brother and figures the dog's in good hands while she's handling all the fallout."

On the surface, that sounded like a logical

enough scenario, although I wasn't certain how Adelaide could know for sure that Lexi was being watched by a reliable person. Yes, I'd told Chief Stanton that I fostered animals, but it wasn't as if I had a website with lots of glowing testimonials or anything to back up my story. All the work I did with witches' familiars wasn't something I advertised, except for my cover story about fostering them so people wouldn't get too curious about the menagerie I tended to host on a continual basis.

Better not to worry about it too much. I'd deal with Adelaide when she contacted me. For now, the situation seemed mostly stable.

And as much as I would have liked to discuss the mysterious witch who'd confronted Milton about her missing book so I could get Noah's insights on the situation, I knew I'd have to keep my lip zipped on that topic. There was no way I could adequately explain how I'd gotten access to that information without divulging that I'd seen some of it in a scrying mirror and had a magically talking dog describe the rest, so I left it alone.

"If you're still trying to dig up some more details," Noah said, "maybe you should talk to that detective here in Salem. Falco, right?"

I'd been in the middle of taking a sip of my iced tea, and it took every ounce of willpower I possessed not to do a spit take. Somehow, I managed to swallow the tea without incident, so I was able to say, "Do you know him?"

"We're not best friends or anything," Noah replied with a grin. "But I've worked with some of the dogs in the police department's K-9 unit, and I met him one time when he came by with one of the other officers to get the dog I'd been treating. Anyway, he seems like a good guy. Maybe he'd be willing to do some asking around. You can tell him I sent you."

Once again, by sheer force of will, I was somehow able to keep my face from betraying me. "Oh, really?" I said, doing my best to appear the picture of innocence. "Maybe I'll try looking into that. I just don't want him to think I'm trying to interfere or something."

"I doubt he'll think that," Noah replied, then took another bite of sandwich. "Especially since you're watching the murder victim's dog. It's kind of natural that you'd want to be kept in the loop."

I hadn't really looked at the situation from that angle, but he had a point. And since Derek and I hadn't had much contact since the investigation into Anna Warren's death was wrapped up, I had to hope he understood that things were serious with Noah and me and that I was reaching out to him in a professional capacity and nothing more.

"All right," I said, hoping I didn't sound too reluctant. Yes, it made sense to contact the one and only person I knew in the Salem P.D., but I couldn't help feeling awkward about it. "I'll try to give Detective Falco a call after lunch. It's possible he won't be able to help out since the murder didn't take place in his jurisdiction, but I suppose I won't know if I don't ask."

"Exactly," Noah replied, and took another bite of his sandwich. He looked blissfully unaware that he'd just thrown a major complication into my life, but because I'd already agreed to contact Derek, there wasn't much I could do about it now.

Except hope the detective was now dating someone and couldn't care less about me.

Chapter 7

Heart of the Matter

Noah had to leave a little before one. We shared a hearty salami-flavored kiss, and he told me he'd come by after work.

"Do you need me to bring takeout?"

Since he'd already fed me twice in a row...well, all right, almost, since he hadn't brought me breakfast...I felt it was now my duty to step up.

"No, it's fine," I said. "I'll figure something out."

"All right," he replied, then gave me a quick kiss on the cheek and hurried down the front steps. He'd lingered a bit longer than he probably should, and I knew he needed to move fast so he wouldn't miss his one o'clock appointment.

The house felt a little flatter, a little emptier, after he left, which I told myself was silly. I had the two dogs there with me, although, since they'd gotten more Italian sliced meats than they probably should, they'd decided to go outside and lie in the sun and sleep it off.

Which left me to get the chicken out of the freezer and set it in some cold water in one side of the sink to thaw. The timing might be a little tight, but I thought I should still be able to get dinner on the table by seven without too much trouble.

A quick text to Sage to see how things were going at the store—smooth and quiet, according to her reply—and then I knew I didn't have much else that I absolutely had to do. I supposed I could have dug around online, trying to find more information about Milton Keyes or maybe his sister Adelaide, but really, I knew I'd probably have much better luck reaching out to Derek Falco.

Something I really, really didn't want to do.

Just get it over with, I told myself. *Chances are, he'll tell you he can't help and that'll be the end of it.*

Or so I hoped.

I didn't have his contact information stored on my phone, but I'd kept the business card he'd given me all those months ago when I was trying to figure out who had murdered Milo's mistress. The card was jammed into the junk drawer in my desk, but after rooting my way past pencils and Post-Its and some stray rubber bands, I found it smashed toward the back.

A deep breath, and then I made myself enter

the digits for his phone number, all the while hoping I'd get his voicemail. True, I didn't have any clear idea as to what I planned to leave as a message, but I still thought it would be easier than talking to him directly.

As luck would have it, he picked up on the second ring. "Detective Falco, Salem P.D."

Great. "Um...hi, Derek. It's Charity Hughes."

Maybe the briefest startled silence. Then he said, "Oh, hi, Charity. What can I do for you?"

No asking me how I was or anything like that, which I supposed was to be expected. After my radio silence the past two months, he must have guessed I wasn't calling just to catch up.

"I was hoping you could do me a favor."

Obviously, I couldn't see his face, but I had to believe he wasn't thrilled to hear these words. "What kind of favor?"

Might as well jump in with both feet. "Did you hear about the man who was killed in Dunstable, Milton Keyes?"

"Yes."

That was his only reply. His tone was guarded, which told me he probably already knew what I was about to ask but wanted to hear me say it anyway.

"I—well, it's kind of a long story, but I'm fostering his dog. Chief Stanton from the Dunstable P.D. told me he would be in touch if he needed to talk to me about anything else. I haven't heard anything from him, though, so I was sort of hoping you might be able to get me some information about what's going on, if only so I know how long I might need to keep Lexi. She's a chihuahua and doesn't eat the same kind of food as my dog Milo, and...."

That wasn't even a lie. I did need to go into town and get some supplies for the little dog, because what Noah had given me from his vet clinic would run out tomorrow sometime.

When Derek replied, his tone sounded a little softer, a little less guarded. "That was nice of you to take her in. But how did she end up with you when she lives so far away?"

That's something we'd all like to know, I thought. However, I only said, "Someone dumped her at Collins Cove Park here in Salem. I have no idea why. But Noah asked me to watch her because it was his neighbor who brought her to his clinic."

"Ah."

A single syllable, one that didn't tell me very much. For all I knew, Derek had responded that way because my previous reply had let him know I was still very much with Noah Jenkins.

Before I could figure out what I should say in response, though, Derek went on, "That's a tough position to be in. It's good of you to be taking care of the dog."

"Well, it's kind of what I do."

"True. Anyway, let me make a few calls and see what I can dig up. That's not my jurisdiction, but I went to college with one of the guys on the Dunstable force, and he might be able to tell me a few things. Just hang tight, and I'll get back to you as soon as I can."

I would have made a "small world" comment, but after all, Massachusetts was a small state with a lot of interconnections. Witches tended to stay put in the towns where they were born and didn't mingle as much as most people did, and yet I'd noticed a lot of mundanes from around here tended to stick close to home, too.

"Thanks, Derek," I said. "I really appreciate it."

"Not a problem. I'll be in touch when I find out something."

He ended the call there, and I set my phone down on the desktop. Now it looked like a waiting game.

However, I didn't intend to wait for Derek to call me back before I ran my errand to the pet store. Even if Adelaide Hanford turned up on my doorstep tonight and demanded that I hand over her brother's dog, I could just give her the food to take with her. Unless she also had a small dog of her own, I doubted she'd have the right thing to feed Lexi.

First, though, I needed to find out what that even was.

An hour later, I was back home, well-stocked with Science Diet in both wet and dry forms, along with some bacon apple treats that weren't anything Lexi had specified but which I thought she might like… and Milo, too, although they were tiny and he could probably have swallowed a handful of the things without batting an eye.

Nothing from Derek, though, and I told myself I needed to be patient. I'd made my request out of the blue, after all, and he probably had plenty of his own work to handle before he could even think about contacting his college buddy on the Dunstable police force.

Still, I wasn't used to having barely anything to do. The few times I'd stayed home from work when I should have been at the store were because I was sick or, as had happened too frequently over the summer, I had some kind of crazy murder investigation to deal with.

Well, I supposed I was dealing with one now, but because I couldn't proceed until I heard back from Derek, I was effectively stymied.

However, he finally called a little after five, just

as I was about to pull the chicken out of its cold water bath and start prepping it to go in the oven.

"Sorry about the delay," he said. "I had something come up here at work, and Phil wasn't answering his phone for a while."

"That's fine," I assured him. "I know you're busy."

A muffled sound that I thought might have been one of assent. "Anyway, Phil says they're trying to downplay the situation because if the details got out, the tabloids would be all over it."

"'The tabloids'?" I repeated. "What, was Milton Keyes having a torrid affair with a movie star or something?"

Derek chuckled, but I couldn't detect much humor in the sound. "Not the celebrity tabloids. I'm talking about the kind of papers that like to publish stories about gruesome murders."

"What was so gruesome about it?" I asked then, frowning. True, stumbling onto any kind of murder scene was fairly traumatic, but it wasn't as if I'd found Mr. Keyes chopped into bits and stored in Tupperware containers in his refrigerator. "Wasn't he stabbed?"

A pause. "You probably couldn't see much from where you were standing. Just a lot of blood, right?"

"Yes, there was blood," I replied. Lots and lots

of blood, dark and viscous against the equally dark wood floors. It hadn't been a pretty sight, but....

"Turns out whoever killed him didn't just stab him in the heart. They physically removed it."

Right then, I was very glad that hours and hours had passed since lunch. Even so, a sour taste flooded my mouth, and I gulped down bile.

"That's...horrible," I managed.

"Yes, it was pretty gruesome. And it's gone—whoever did this, they took the heart with them. Some kind of trophy, I guess."

Somehow, I made my way over to one of the kitchen chairs so I could sit down, since I wasn't sure whether my suddenly rubbery knees would hold me up. "But...why?"

Another of those pauses, as if Derek was trying to figure out exactly how much he should say. "Anyone who does something like that is sick. Maybe not in a way that's obvious to everyone around them, but it's not the sort of thing that a normal, functioning member of society would do. They could have had a grudge against the guy, or they could've randomly targeted him because they thought he'd be easy to use for their trophy collecting, thanks to the way he lived alone. I honestly don't know. But everyone on the Dunstable force is pretty shaken up by the whole thing."

I could imagine. It was the sort of picture-perfect, prosperous village that came to mind when people tried to envision the ideal Massachusetts town, and I seriously doubted anyone on the force there had had to deal with a single crime that even began to approach this one in terms of pure viciousness. "It's awful," I agreed.

"They sent the body to Boston for the autopsy," Derek continued. "Sounds like they're going over it with a fine-tooth comb, which I completely understand. If there's even the slightest chance that this wasn't a one-off kind of murder and the killer might strike again, Chief Stanton wants to make sure they recover whatever kind of physical evidence they can."

Even though the kitchen was warm enough—I'd already started preheating the oven—I couldn't hold back the shiver that traced its way down my spine. Deep down, I knew Bill Stanton didn't have much to worry about, that this had been a targeted killing. The image of the dark-haired witch flashed into my mind, even though I only knew what she looked like in profile.

Had she been the one who'd stabbed Milton Keyes in the chest, who had cut his heart out?

I didn't want to believe any woman could be capable of that kind of violence, but I knew better. The history of witchcraft had some very dark chapters, although I liked to think no one I knew practiced such terrible magic.

Well, except one.

No, that was ridiculous. Elise Figg had done some dubious things in her life, but I couldn't believe she was capable of carving someone's heart out of his chest.

Putting my worries about her use of dark magic aside, how would she even have known Milton Keyes?

"…couldn't find out anything about the sister," Derek was saying, and I managed to jerk my attention back to the here and now. "So it's probably a good thing you're going to stock up supplies for the dog."

"I went this afternoon and got some things for her," I said, knowing my voice sounded way too tight. "But thanks for checking. I assume Chief Stanton gave Milton's sister my contact information, so now I just need to wait to hear from her."

"Well, hang in there," Derek told me. "I'm sure she'll reach out to you eventually. A lot of loose ends kind of get neglected when family members have to deal with a sudden death."

I supposed so, although I didn't really want to think of Lexi as a "loose end." Milo was like family to me, and I had to believe Milton had looked at his little long-haired chihuahua the same way, considering how he seemed to have taken her almost everywhere with him.

"She's fine here for as long as necessary," I said firmly. "But thanks again for looking into this."

"No problem," Derek replied. He must have gotten the sense that I wanted to get off the phone, because he added, "I'll let you know if I hear anything else. Take care."

The call ended there, and I set my cell phone down on the kitchen table. While I supposed it helped to have gained some additional information, I couldn't stop thinking about the way Milton Keyes had died.

What if he'd still been alive when his assailant cut his heart out of his chest?

As quickly as I could, I banished that terrible image from my mind. No, he'd been stabbed, and then after he was dead, the murderer had gone on with her...or his...grisly business. While I immediately suspected the witch I'd seen in the scrying mirror, I couldn't know for sure that she was the one responsible for Milton's murder. The encounter in the bookstore might have been a random incident and nothing more.

I knew one thing, though. As much as I would have liked to avoid such a conversation, I realized I really needed to talk to Elise Figg about all this.

Elise was a few years younger than my mother. Like my mother—and a lot of witches in general—she had one daughter, Sorcha, who was six years my junior and currently attending Boston University. The house where they lived was down the street from the home where I'd grown up, and nearly as familiar to me as my own. However, Elise's style was very different from my mother's...or mine...and had always felt like the exact opposite of the sort of interior design style a witch should prefer, with mid-century furniture and very few accessories and not a thing out of place.

I'd left Milo and Lexi behind, admonishing them to stay in the house while I was gone—and placing a few extra protection spells on the place before I left, just to be safe. No, I hadn't seen any indication that anyone was stalking me or trying to get the dog back, but after hearing the gruesome details of Milton Keyes' death, I figured it was better to be safe.

Now I sat in Elise's smoothly modern living room, sipping from a cup of oolong while she eyed me with some curiosity. In contrast to the sleek interiors of her house, she always dressed in a kind of boho style, with lots of Indian-print skirts and silver jewelry, even when the weather might have demanded something a little heavier. When I'd called to see if I could come over, I'd only said it was to ask about a certain point of dark magic, and although she'd seemed startled, she hadn't told me that was the sort of thing she wouldn't discuss.

"Why would a murderer cut out their victim's heart?" I blurted, and she raised an eyebrow.

"Are you asking in general, or in magical terms?"

"Well, both, I guess," I replied. "I don't know for sure whether the murderer here is a witch. I only have suspicions."

Elise sipped from her cup of tea. "Then why don't you tell me what you know, and then we can go from there."

No point in hesitating; this was why I'd come over here, after all. Another swallow of fragrant tea to give me some courage, and then I launched into the whole story—how Lexi had been found in the park and I'd taken her in, how I'd discovered where she lived and had taken her there to reunite her with her master.

How I'd found Milton Keyes dead on the floor.

Through all of it, Elise was silent, apparently content to let me speak my piece and get it over with. When I was done, though, she set her cup down on the simple black ceramic coaster in front of her and folded her hands on her knees, skin pale against her skirt with its warm autumn shades of brown and gold and russet.

What she said next surprised me.

"Why haven't you spoken to your mother about any of this?"

A guilty pang went through me. It was true I'd

reached out to Grace and now Elise for help, rather than calling my mother, but that was simply because this wasn't her area of expertise. She was an accomplished kitchen witch and had a handy arsenal of other domestic tricks up her magical sleeve, and wasn't someone with a huge knowledge of witch history or dark magic, the way my two other coven members were.

Still, I'd gotten embroiled in yet another mystery through no fault of my own, and I supposed I probably should have gotten in contact just to let my mother know what was going on.

"I guess it slipped my mind," I said, and Elise smiled.

"Well, you should still talk to her at some point," she said. "Just to keep her up to date." I nodded, and Elise went on, "It's not any kind of magic I've practiced, and I don't know anyone who would be willing to do something so terrible. The police in Dunstable might be calling it murder, but more properly, what we're dealing with here is human sacrifice."

My eyes flared open at that remark. "But—"

"I know," Elise broke in, although gently. "The common belief is that human sacrifice was practiced to appease the gods or to enlist their help in some sort of magical workings. We all know that gods don't exist, but there are still dark powers in the universe, ones most witches know to leave alone, since they're far too difficult to control. All I can think is that this witch—the one you've caught glimpses of, even though you don't know who she is—decided she wanted something so badly she was willing to throw caution aside and practice some of the very darkest magic that exists in order to get it."

What did she want, though? What could be so important that she was ready to step across such a terrible line?

"Lexi said something about a book," I said slowly, and Elise gave a knowing nod.

"It sounds like our witch is on the hunt for a grimoire," she said.

"I thought those were just myths," I returned. Yes, all witches had books where they wrote down their spells and kept track of potion ingredients and that kind of thing, but grimoires were a different kind of magic entirely, compendiums of dark, powerful enchantments centuries old. They had always seemed like more of the witch form of the boogeyman than anything that was actually real.

Elise reached for her cup of tea, then picked it up and sipped from it. To look at her, you'd think we were only discussing the weather, not powerful magic that had existed before the mists of time.

"All myths have a grain of truth," she said. "I've never seen a grimoire or even heard of one being here in the United States, but it sounds as if this particular witch is on the trail of one and is willing to do whatever she has to in order to get her hands on it."

A little trickle of cold moved down my spine. This was a new and extremely unpleasant wrinkle in a case that was already gruesome enough. "So, why make Lexi talk?" I asked next. "What does that have to do with finding the grimoire?"

Elise's shoulders lifted. "I have no idea. The only thing I can think of is that the dog had seen or heard something she hadn't understood at the time, and the witch cast the spell of speech on her to see if she would give up her secret. She must not have gotten what she wanted and decided to dispose of the dog."

"Why not dump her closer to home?"

For the first time, Elise appeared almost perplexed. "I'm not sure," she said. "I'll admit that part of the story doesn't make much sense to me. The only thing I can think of is that possibly someone else was after the dog, and the witch decided to dump her far enough away that it would be more difficult to track her down." A flicker in her gray eyes then, as if she'd thought of something unpleasant, and she sipped some more tea.

"What?" I demanded after she stayed silent for an uncomfortable moment or two.

"I'm just guessing here," she said. "But it occurred to me that maybe the dog was dumped here because the witch hoped she would end up in your hands. After all, most witches know about Charity Hughes, the familiar whisperer. It could be she thought you might be able to get information out of the dog that she couldn't. At the same time, she wouldn't want to risk you seeing her or catching even a whiff of her magic, which explains why Lexi might have been dropped off at the park rather than on your doorstep."

Oh, no...I didn't like that idea at all. However, I had to admit that Elise's theory had some merit. It wasn't as if I was anything close to a celebrity in the witch world—unlike my friend Stella, who'd been a champion Witch Olympics broomstick rider until she'd retired and started a family with her frost-elf husband, Kai—but people knew about me, knew I was a resource they could use if they started having trouble with their animal companions.

"Lexi hasn't told me anything about a book," I said. "At least, nothing except the argument Milton had with the witch in his antique store. I have no idea where it could even be. The dog said it wasn't in the shop."

"Possibly, it's in his house," Elise suggested.

"That's way too obvious," I replied at once. "If the person who killed him had suspected it of being there, they would have torn the place apart looking for it. When I was there, though, the house was spotless. Nothing was out of place."

These objections didn't seem to bother Elise at all. Wearing a faint smile, she asked, "Did you see the whole house?"

Well, of course I hadn't. There hadn't been any reason for me to go upstairs, not after I made that grisly discovery in the family room.

I shook my head, and Elise's eyebrows raised slightly.

"Then you can't have any idea as to what might have been going on in the rooms on the second floor," she said. "It's possible Milton Keyes hid the grimoire up there."

"If he did, then the witch must have discovered it," I said. "I mean, Milton was no witch, obviously. He couldn't have put a concealment spell or an illusion spell on it. The thing would have been easy enough to find."

"Possibly," Elise allowed. "Or possibly not. But it's something that bears looking into."

While she had a point, I didn't see how I'd be allowed into the place. For all I knew, it was still an active crime scene. Even if it wasn't, I doubted Chief Stanton would allow me to just waltz in there.

Then again, I was a witch. In general, we didn't have to ask for permission for that sort of thing.

"Okay," I said, knowing even as I spoke how reluctant I sounded. "I guess it's time for me to take a second look at Mr. Keyes' house."

Chapter 8

Grim Dark

Obviously, I couldn't tell Noah what I was up to. While I had no doubt he'd watch Milo and Lexi for me, I thought it better to kill two birds with one stone...in this case, calling my mother and asking her to dog-sit, and also letting her know what was going on.

She didn't seem too pleased that I'd gotten embroiled in yet another murder mystery, but at least she hadn't said no and had instead told me she'd be over in the next fifteen minutes.

While I was waiting for her, I let Milo and Lexi know I needed to go out again but that my mother was coming over to watch them since Noah was still at work. Milo had already met my mother and they'd gotten along well, so I didn't think having her keep an eye on the dogs was going to be a problem. Lexi had looked a little dubious at first, but

Milo assured her that my mother was lots of fun and she'd take good care of them.

All the same, I noticed the sidelong glance he sent me, one that seemed to signal he understood some danger might be lurking and that was why I'd decided to have my mother play dog-sitter now. I gave him a very small nod, one he returned at once, as if he knew I expected him to watch over Lexi as well.

When my mother arrived, she patted Milo on the head and exclaimed over and over how cute Lexi was, something guaranteed to win the chihuahua's affection almost at once. The little dog let my mother scratch behind her ears and in that important spot in the middle of her back, winning her over at once.

"I won't be gone long," I said. "But there's something I need to check on."

My mother's eyes, a clear green almost identical to mine, searched my face. "I hope you're not putting yourself in danger, Charity."

"No more than I have to," I replied lightly. To be honest, even though Elise had told me it was important to search Milton Keyes's house, I wasn't sure whether I'd find anything of note there. Derek hadn't told me how long Milton had been dead when I stumbled across him, which meant the unknown witch...if she really was the killer...might have had plenty of time to search the house and make off with the grimoire.

If it had even been there in the first place.

"All right," my mother said, in the sort of resigned tone that told me she didn't approve of me poking around in places I shouldn't but wasn't going to try to dissuade me. I had to admit, after I'd had her over for dinner a while back so she could meet Noah, she'd gotten a lot mellower. For some reason, I'd thought the meeting would make her pressure me that much more to get serious with him, but in fact, the opposite had happened. It was almost as if, once she'd seen us together, she could tell things already were serious and she didn't want to do anything to jeopardize our relationship.

"I'm not sure how long I'll be," I said. "But I'm hoping it won't be more than an hour at the most."

Which would give me plenty of time to get home before dinner. Noah and I hadn't made any concrete plans for tonight, and yet I had a feeling he'd want to come over to check on Lexi. Well, and see me and Milo, but that was sort of a given.

"I'll make sure everything stays calm here," my mother assured me.

Between her and Milo, I thought I had everything handled. I thanked her, told the dogs I wouldn't be gone very long, and then left them in the living room so I could go into the kitchen and fetch my broom from its usual resting place in the corner near the pantry.

To be honest, I wasn't the world's best broomstick rider. However, even I could get from place to place a lot faster on a broom than I would driving, and traveling by broomstick meant I could land somewhere near Milton's house, cast one of my "don't look at me" spells, and sneak into the house to take a peek at what was going on upstairs.

Of course, my plan would only work if the police had closed out the crime scene and left the place empty. Those spells of distracting people so they wouldn't notice me didn't work very well at close quarters.

Only one way to find out, I supposed. I cast the first "look away" spell so I could be sure my neighbors weren't paying any attention as I took to the air, then headed west toward Dunstable. The landscape flashed by beneath me, with some maples and oaks and elms already starting to put on their bright autumn shades of red and amber and yellow. In addition to the "don't look at me" spell, I'd also employed my usual invisible net to make sure bugs stayed out of my way, and another to ensure I wouldn't get too cold flying a thousand feet above the ground.

Soon enough, I passed the turnoff for Dunstable, following Main Street until I took a right above Highland Street. A moment later, I'd descended behind the shelter of the garage so I could take a quick survey of my surroundings...and also disguised my broomstick as a collapsible umbrella, just in case. It was still a somewhat conspicuous item for me to be carrying, especially on such a clear, sunny day, but it was always easier to use an illusion that was close to the original item's form factor whenever possible.

As far as I could tell, the property was deserted. Yellow police tape blocked the garage doors, and when I went around back, more yellow tape crossed the French door into the family room, but it looked to me as though the Dunstable police had finished their investigation and locked up the place.

Perfect.

I laid my hand on the door handle, muttered an unlocking spell, and pushed my way past the police tape.

It was dark inside. I blinked at the contrast from the bright, sunny day outdoors, then reached for a light switch. Since all the blinds were closed, I doubted anyone would be able to tell I'd turned the lights on, and I needed to see what I was doing.

As before, the house looked neat and tidy enough...well, except for the dark blotch against the hardwood floor in the family room, black against deep brown. Would anything get that out, or would the floor in that room need to be replaced?

Honestly, if I were the person who bought the house...I assumed Milton's sister would have to put it on the market at some point...then I wouldn't want to be walking across a floor where someone had died.

But that would happen on some hazy day off in the future. For now, I had other matters to occupy me.

Now that I looked around, I could tell the place wasn't quite as tidy as it had been when I discovered Milton's body. Whitish dust on the countertops and other surfaces seemed to show where the police had been looking for fingerprints, and a couple of cupboard doors had been left open. I took note of where everything was so I wouldn't disturb anything or leave any trace of my presence here, then went farther into the family room.

It was a large space open to the kitchen, with big windows that probably afforded a stunning view of the backyard. Now, though, with all the shutters closed, it just felt gloomy, despite the cheerful plaid couch and the large built-in on one wall that looked as if it had been custom-designed for the space to hide the big TV I could just barely see shining from inside its cabinet.

Books filled both sides of the built-in, so I hurried over to take a look at them in case the grimoire might have been hidden there next to a copy of Stephen King's *1963* or David Foster

Wallace's *Infinite Jest.* However, nothing I saw appeared remotely suspicious. No, it was just a collection of hardbacks filed neatly by author last name, with all the spines facing proudly out rather than following that recent ridiculous—to my eyes, anyway—trend of turning books around so they'd present a unified beige front to the room.

But maybe the grimoire had a spell of illusion set on it to make it look like an ordinary hardback. My talents in this area weren't the strongest, but I knew I had to make the attempt.

In whispers lost and time's soft shroud,
Reveal thy form, once veiled, now proud.
Among the silent kin you hide,
Emerge by spell, no more to bide.

Nothing happened, but that didn't tell me much. Either all these books were no more than they seemed, or my spell had failed. Whatever was going on, I didn't see anything different here, which meant I needed to keep looking.

I'd passed the living and dining rooms so quickly on my first foray here that I couldn't remember much about either space except they'd both been furnished with gorgeous antiques. A more measured survey now showed I'd remembered the antiques correctly, but there definitely weren't any books in either room. There didn't seem to be any bedrooms on this level, which meant I needed to head upstairs.

Something about climbing the wide, graceful steps put me on edge, although I couldn't really say why. Maybe it was just that the second floor generally tended to contain the more private sections of a house, the places where people slept and dreamed and showered and made love.

But since I'd come all the way here, I needed to keep it together and do what I needed to do. It might turn out that this had all been a colossal waste of time, and yet I knew I'd kick myself if I didn't check every corner, every closet.

Upstairs, it looked as though there were five bedrooms, three on one side and two on the other, with a bathroom on my left as I entered the corridor. It was large and appeared as though it had been recently updated, but no books in there, either.

One bedroom looked like it was intended as a guest room, although something told me no one had actually ever slept there. It felt more like Milton Keyes had thought there should be a spare room, so he'd decorated one that way, with a queen-size bed and a highboy and two pretty Hepplewhite side tables.

The bedroom next door appeared to be his office, since it had a desk with a big iMac sitting on it, a couple of dark wood file cabinets, and not much else. Had the police tried to get into the computer, or had they left it as-is because they didn't think it had anything to do with their murder investigation?

I had no way of knowing...well, not without asking questions that would probably attract more attention to me than I would have liked...so I told myself to ignore the computer for now. It wasn't as if I could hack my way into it. Magic could do a lot of amazing things, but I'd never used it to gain access to someone else's hardware and didn't think I could even if I wanted to.

No bookcases in there, though, so I moved down to the next room.

Jackpot.

Milton had clearly set up this space as a library, since its only furniture was custom bookcases that lined every wall, with a big wing chair in the middle and a small table next to it, just the perfect size to hold a cup of tea or coffee as you read. Every single shelf was crammed with books, which meant I would probably be in here for a while.

I ran my hand along every single spine, trying to see if I could sense whether any of those hardbacks of various sizes felt different to my fingertips than it looked to my eyes. They all seemed to be exactly what they appeared to be, though, and I found myself frowning as I went along.

It was sure seeming more and more to me that the grimoire had never been here at all.

Don't give up, I told myself and kept going, feeling each book carefully, forcing myself not to hurry even though I could sense time ticking by. Yes, my return trip by broomstick wouldn't take me very long, but still, if I lingered here much past five, I ran the risk of Noah dropping by the house while my mother was still there. I had no doubt that she'd be able to manufacture some sort of plausible explanation as to why she was watching the two dogs while I was off running an errand, but it would be a lot easier if I could just get out of here promptly and forestall any awkwardness.

Well, none of the books felt like they were anything except what they were supposed to be, which meant it was time for another spell.

In whispers soft and sight unseen,
Reveal the tome where magic dreams.
Amongst the many, stand alone,
Guide my hand to what's unknown.

And again nothing. For all I knew, the grimoire had the kind of spell placed on it that would repel any magic that sought to reveal its identity, although those sorts of enchantments were difficult to cast and even harder to maintain for any length of time. No, it seemed much more likely to me that the grimoire had been hidden elsewhere.

In fact, I was starting to wonder if Milton Keyes had never possessed the book at all. It didn't seem too implausible that the witch who'd hidden it had made it sound as if the grimoire was in his keeping in order to throw anyone who might be looking for it off the scent.

And if that was the case, then he'd been killed for nothing.

Not for nothing, I reminded myself. *You still don't know exactly what kind of spell the witch was going to use his heart for.*

Or maybe....

Maybe the witch had killed Milton Keyes in a fit of anger when she realized he didn't have the book here, and then had come back and carved out his heart when she realized she could use it in the sort of dark ritual necessary to track down the grimoire.

For some reason, that thought made the crime seem even worse, although I couldn't exactly articulate why.

But right now all I was doing was speculating... and wasting time. Even though an entire library of books surrounded me, not a single one of them was the grimoire, which meant I needed to keep going.

The fourth bedroom was empty except for an antique dresser. It looked like Milton had had plans for this room but hadn't yet carried them out...and never would.

I blew out a breath and made myself walk over to the last door, the one I knew must open on the master bedroom. For some reason, I really didn't want to go inside, didn't want to intrude on the personal space of a man who would never sleep there again.

No choice, though.

I opened the door and then stood on the threshold, mouth agape.

It looked as if an entire army of whirling dervishes had gone through there, pulling underwear and socks out of drawers, knocking the mattress askew, flinging the contents of the walk-in closet all over the floor.

Somehow I doubted the police had done any of this.

No, it had to have been the witch, coming back to finish searching the place after the police had concluded their investigation. Since I had no idea when that might have happened, I couldn't begin to guess how recently she might have been here.

Or maybe she was still somewhere close by.

Heart pounding, I turned and glanced back down the hallway, but I was alone. Then again, some witches were very good at turning themselves invisible.

She would have attacked you the second you

walked inside if she was still anywhere around, I told myself, and my jangled nerves stopped twanging just the slightest bit.

However, I'd managed to effectively creep myself out, and I knew I wouldn't be able to really relax until I was safely out of here and mounted on my broom and heading home.

Although all my instincts were telling me to get the hell back to Salem, I made myself go over to the closet and peek inside. A few suits and shirts still hung there, but the majority of them were either strewn on the floor inside or scattered around the rest of the bedroom. Even the orderly shoe organizer that took up the back wall of the closet had been pulled down, with wingtips and penny loafers and deck shoes of all descriptions tossed everywhere.

Whoever had done this, they obviously hadn't been very happy.

No books here, though, and none in the *en suite* bathroom, which had been similarly ransacked. I waded through the detritus and made my way back to the main part of the bedroom, where I looked under the bed just to be safe. Nothing there except one forlorn Topsider. God only knows where its mate had ended up.

"Well, so much for that," I said aloud, and wished I hadn't. Something about hearing the sound of my voice in the trashed bedroom made me uneasy all over again, as if I couldn't quite rid myself of the sensation that someone...or something...still lurked nearby, watching everything I did and everything I said.

Time to get out of there. I hadn't learned anything, except that somebody had come back to the house after the police left, desperate to find the grimoire. I had no idea where it might be, except that I doubted it was anywhere inside Milton Keyes' home.

I made my way back downstairs, retrieving my disguised broom from the spot where I'd left it lying on the kitchen counter. Once again, I glanced around and wondered if there was something I'd missed, a single detail or item out of place that might have led me to the right location to find the grimoire.

But nothing spoke to me, and I shook my head. Maybe once I had the chance to get away and ponder everything I'd seen, some kind of clue might jump out at me, but for now, it seemed best to go home and regroup.

Umbrella-broom dangling from my left hand, I went to the French doors off the family room. I'd barely laid my fingers on the handle when the door swung inward, and a pair of shocked eyes met mine.

"Who the hell are you?" Adelaide Hanford demanded.

Chapter 9

Sisterhood

A million lies jumped to my lips, none of which sounded remotely plausible. All right, I'd just have to tell the truth.

Well, some of it, anyway.

"I'm Charity Hughes," I said. "I'm watching Lexi."

Adelaide Hanford was tall like her brother had been, at least three inches more than my modest five foot five. She glared down at me, one patrician eyebrow lifted at a caustic angle. "If you're here, then who's watching the dog?"

"My mother," I replied immediately. Again, nothing more than the truth, and something of the angry light in Adelaide's eyes dimmed slightly.

Not all the way, though. Not even close.

"How did you get in?"

"The door wasn't locked," I lied. "I think

maybe someone forgot to close up properly when the police left."

Her lips thinned. "Maybe," she allowed. "And I'll definitely follow up with Bill Stanton about that. However, it doesn't explain why you're inside my brother's house, or why you would have driven all this way without knowing for sure whether you'd be able to get in at all."

Fair point. It felt beyond awkward to be confronting one another like this right on the threshold to the family room, so I backed out of the way so she could come inside.

Which she did, although her mouth compressed even further as she caught sight of the dark blotch on the wood floor.

"I came over here because I wanted to get some food for Lexi," I explained, thinking furiously. "I got some from the vet who rescued her, but it wasn't sitting well, and I knew she'd do better with the food she was used to. There wasn't anyone I could ask about that, so I thought I'd come to the house and see if the police investigators were still here and could let me in."

For a moment, Adelaide Hanford surveyed me coldly, and I did my best to meet her gaze squarely, looking as guileless as possible. I'd only just met her, but she gave the distinct impression of a woman who was used to having people jump when she told them how high.

Unfortunately for her, I'd never been someone like that. Under different circumstances, I might have had a few choice words to say about her high-handed attitude, but right now, I knew I needed to act as nonthreatening...and believable...as possible.

"Obviously, the police weren't here," she observed, her tone dry.

"No," I agreed. I wouldn't say she'd softened exactly, only that she seemed a teeny bit less hostile than she had the moment before. "I was going to drive to the station to see if I could have someone come back over here with me, but then I had the crazy idea to try the back door. It opened, so I figured I'd just pop in, grab the dog food, and then go home."

"Then where's the dog food?" Adelaide asked.

Oh, hell. I'd never even gone looking for it, obviously, because fetching provisions for Lexi hadn't been my reason for being here at all.

And that meant I needed to lie some more and hope for the best.

"I couldn't find any," I said. "Maybe Mr. Keyes left her food somewhere else, like the laundry room or something. I didn't get that far, though—since I couldn't find it here in the kitchen and didn't think it was right to go snooping around the house, I decided I should just go home."

Adelaide's eyes narrowed again, but I got the impression she didn't know where her brother had kept Lexi's food any more than I did. "If you drove here, then where's your car?"

Damn, did this woman work for the FBI or something?

Since it wasn't very likely that I'd taken a bus to get to Milton's house—were there even buses that went to tiny Dunstable?—I had to settle for another lie.

"I had a friend drive me," I said. "She dropped me off while she went to get some coffee. She should be back any time now."

Not the greatest story in the world, but because it didn't seem as if anyone in this neighborhood parked their cars on the street, I couldn't exactly claim one of them as mine and hope for the best.

"I see," Adelaide said, her tone turning icy again. "Well, since you're currently trespassing on my dead brother's property, I'll have to ask you to leave and hope you meet your friend coming back from her coffee run. I suppose I could turn you in to Chief Stanton, but since you're watching Milton's dog, I'll let it go."

The words "for now" hung ominously in the air, and I swallowed.

Still, I couldn't quite leave things there.

"What about Lexi?"

"What about her?" Adelaide returned.

"Do you want me to keep watching her? Or should we make arrangements for you to take her?"

The other woman's nostrils flared in dislike. "You can have her," she said coldly. "Frankly, I could never see why my brother was so besotted with that little rat of a dog."

What a b—

Somehow, I managed to keep about a thousand angry words from flying out of my mouth. "She's a sweet dog," I said calmly, even as I seethed with the kind of rage that did my red hair justice. "I'm very glad to have her."

And before Adelaide could reply, I pushed my way through the French doors and into the backyard. It wasn't until I'd rounded a corner of the house that I realized I'd had my disguised broom clutched in my left hand the whole time.

Well, if Milton's sister wanted to think me crazy for walking around holding a collapsible umbrella on a clear day, fine.

Better crazy than mean.

Because I wouldn't put it past Adelaide to keep watch to make sure I really did leave the property, I stalked down the front path to the street—this semi-rural area didn't have sidewalks—and in the direction of Dunstable's minuscule downtown, where its one and only café appeared to be located. However, just as soon as I'd gone around a curve and was shielded by trees, I cast another "don't look at me spell," popped my broom out to full size, took to the air, and headed for home.

The whole way, though, I was fuming.

How in the world could Adelaide Hanford have said such horrible things about a sweet dog like Lexi?

All right, some people didn't like dogs. But Lexi had obviously been precious to Milton, and one would think his sister would treat her late brother's pet with at least a little kindness and consideration out of respect for his memory if nothing else.

Apparently not.

I didn't doubt for a second that she would have called Chief Stanton to read me the riot act if I hadn't left when she asked. In fact, I thought she might still contact him anyway, just out of spite.

A chill went through me that had nothing to do with the cool air rushing past as I moved over the Massachusetts landscape at a hundred miles per hour. What if Adelaide called the police chief, and he went upstairs and saw the destruction in Milton's bedroom? They'd suspect me immediately, even though she had no concrete evidence that I'd ranged any farther than the kitchen and family room area.

Well, I'd only touched a few things in the house. Also, I'd made sure to cast a minor charm to prevent my fingerprints from lingering on anything I might have picked up, so at least the Dunstable police wouldn't have any physical evidence to connect me to the mess upstairs.

Still, they could make my life difficult for a while if they wanted to. I had no doubt that Derek Falco would vouch for my character if necessary, although I hated to ask him for that kind of favor.

And so I alternately fretted and fumed all the way back to Salem, where I landed in the backyard and hurried into the house. My mother was in the kitchen, sipping from a cup of tea, and sent me a surprised look as I entered. The scent of roast chicken was already starting to fill the air, telling me she'd taken note of the defrosting chicken in the sink and had gone ahead and seasoned it and popped it in the oven so it would be ready around six-thirty.

"Is everything all right?" she asked at once. "You look upset."

"Milton's sister Adelaide caught me poking around the house," I said shortly. "Is there still hot water in the kettle?"

"Yes," my mother replied, expression even more startled. "What did you tell her?"

"That I was there looking for dog food for Lexi," I said. "I think she bought my story, but she's still suspicious. And she's going to be even angrier if she goes upstairs and sees the mess in her brother's bedroom."

My mother's brow furrowed in confusion. "What's the matter with his bedroom?"

"Someone went in there and ransacked the place. I'm sure they were looking for the grimoire, but as far as I can tell, it's nowhere in that house. Still, if Adelaide starts poking around and sees the damage, she's going to think it was me."

Something close to a sigh escaped my mother's lips, but she probably knew better than to say it had been foolish for me to go to Milton's house. Maybe I could have come up with a better plan, and yet I knew I had to make sure the grimoire wasn't in the house somewhere. Now that I'd satisfied myself on that front...well, mostly...I'd deal with the fallout when and if it even happened. Since I didn't know why Adelaide had gone over to her dead brother's house this afternoon, I couldn't know for sure whether she'd felt the need to head upstairs and look around, or whether she'd only wanted to confirm that the police really were done with their investigation and she was now free to do with the house as she pleased.

Or maybe not. I had to believe she was the main beneficiary of his will unless their parents were still alive. Even so, I assumed it would be a while until she could take ownership of the place.

"I'll handle it if that happens," I told my

mother, who now wore an expectant expression on her face, as if she wanted me to offer assurances that I wasn't about to get arrested for breaking and entering, not to mention vandalism. "Besides, I cast a charm so I wouldn't leave any fingerprints or other physical evidence behind, so there's no way the police can prove I caused any of the damage."

"That's something, I suppose," she remarked. "I'd say that you needed to stay out of it, but if there's a dangerous grimoire floating around somewhere unattended, then I think it's all of our problem."

"Which is why I can't exactly let this go," I said. "At least I don't have to worry about Adelaide swooping in to claim Lexi, but—"

"She doesn't want the dog?" my mother cut in, now looking startled again. "But she's such a sweetie."

"She is," I said. "And she and Milo get along great, so it's no problem to keep her."

I spoke firmly on purpose, just so my mother would know I had no intention of fobbing Lexi off on someone else. Yes, it was going to be hard to have a dog who wasn't a familiar, whose life would be much shorter than mine or Milo's, but I swore to myself that I'd love her twice as much to make up the difference.

"They do seem to be good friends already," my mother replied. Because she hadn't offered any arguments, I guessed she'd decided I already had enough on my plate without having to debate whether it was wise for a witch who worked with a variety of familiars to take on a second dog. "And they'll be good company for each other while you're at work."

Oh, damn...work. Yes, I'd had this day to work on the conundrum of Milton Keyes' awful death, but my investigation so far had only turned up more questions. I supposed it was possible I could ask Sage to go it alone again tomorrow, since Wednesdays at the store generally weren't any busier than Tuesdays, and yet I doubted I could stay away much longer than that. True, she'd covered for me on a busy holiday weekend while I was tracking down who had killed Milo's former witch. At the same time, I really didn't want to take that kind of advantage of my assistant. There probably wasn't much chance she'd rage-quit over my request, but still, easygoing as she was, she had her limits just like everyone else.

Well, since I currently didn't have any other leads I needed to follow up on, I didn't see any real reason why I needed to stay home tomorrow... except my undercurrent of worry that whoever had dumped Lexi in Salem might be having second thoughts and might decide to come back and get her.

"That's true," I said in response to my mother's

comment, which was all I felt safe saying right then. At the moment, I didn't want to think about the even darker motive for dropping Lexi here, that maybe whoever was behind all this had done so because they knew she'd end up in my care.

No, that theory had to be the longest of long shots. It wasn't as if Noah was the only vet in Salem, far from it. There had been a very great chance that Lexi might have been taken to one of the town's three other veterinarians, or even handed over to one of our dog rescue groups. If that had happened, I doubted any of them would have brought the dog to me. No, they would have taken care of her on their own while they worked to find her owner.

"Can you watch the dogs tomorrow?" I blurted, and my mother's green eyes opened a little wider.

"Are you worried something might happen to them?"

About all I could do was give a helpless little shrug. "I don't know for sure. There's a whole lot going on here that I don't know. But until I can get a better handle on who was behind this and what their plans were for Lexi, it just seems smarter to have someone keeping an eye on her."

"Then of course I can," my mother replied. "Do you want me to come over here, or would you rather have them come to my house?"

"I'll take them to your place," I said promptly. It just seemed smarter to me to have the dogs off-site in a location where any suspicious characters might not know to look for them. Besides, my mother's yard, while not as big as mine, was large enough to give them plenty of space to roam around and would give them a little change of pace. "I can drop them off on my way to work."

"It'll be fun," she replied. "They were definitely darlings today—we all sat outside in the sun, and then they played a little and came inside to crash on the sofa. I'm surprised they didn't wake up when you came in."

So was I. In fact, the absence of any dogs rushing to greet me made me hurry over to the kitchen entrance so I could peek out into the living room. Sure enough, both dogs were sprawled on the couch, Lexi curled up against Milo with her tiny snout lying against his flank.

The scene made me smile, even as I heaved an inner sigh of relief. I didn't think any witch out there could get past the protection charms I'd set up and my mother's watchful eye, but better to know the dogs were safe and sound.

I turned back to my mother. "Thanks," I said simply, meaning not just the way she'd watched Milo and Lexi but had also taken care of the chicken for me.

Of course, she understood. "That's what I'm here for."

Not long after she left, Noah texted me. *I can still get takeout if you need me to.*

For once, I'd be able to surprise him with a home-cooked meal. He didn't have to know my mother had gotten it started for me.

How about chicken and potatoes? They're already in the oven.

Even better. Need me to bring anything?

Yourself and some wine.

That was my standard response whenever I actually cooked something, which probably didn't happen as often as it should. My mother really had saved the day, both in watching the animals and making sure I wouldn't be eating takeout for the umpteenth time in a row.

See you soon.

I sent back a kiss emoji, and that seemed to be the end of that. Just as I was setting my phone down on the kitchen counter, Milo and Lexi came into the room and gave the air an appreciative sniff.

"Is that chicken?" Lexi asked.

"It is," I replied. "Thanks to my mom, who popped it in the oven for me."

"She's nice," the little dog said, while Milo nodded his agreement.

Most of the time, I thought with an inner grin. However, just because my mother's and my relationship could be sometimes fraught, it didn't mean I planned to mention that to the dogs.

"She is," I said. "And I'm glad to hear you like her, because I'm going to have you stay at her house tomorrow while I go to work."

At once, both dogs' heads tilted in confusion. Even though the situation was serious enough, I couldn't quite help smiling at the comical effect of them moving in unison like that.

"Why?" Milo asked. "Aren't we safe here?"

"I think you are," I said. "But at the same time, I don't want to take any chances. There was some pretty dark magic involved in Milton's death, and I don't want it to affect you any more than it already has."

At once, Lexi's ears swiveled backward. "Dark magic?"

"Nothing you need to worry about," I told her, since I knew there was no way in the world I'd ever divulge what had really happened to her master. "At the same time, though, it just makes sense to take some extra precautions. Besides, you'll like my mom's house. She has comfy furniture and a big yard with a huge oak tree. It'll be fun."

This description seemed to reassure the dogs,

whose tails wagged a little as I spoke. I didn't have a chance to say more, because the doorbell rang then.

Noah must have made it over to the house awfully fast. I had to hope he was okay with hanging out with the dogs for a while so I could get the table set.

I went to the front door and opened it. Standing there wasn't Noah, as I'd thought, but a pair of men wearing dark blue police uniforms.

"Charity Hughes?" one of them asked as he flashed a badge. "We're from the Dunstable police. We need to ask you a few questions."

Chapter 10

Hard Questions

Well, at least the Dunstable P.D.'s police cruiser was new and comfortable. Even so, the ride back to the tiny village felt interminable. Officer Wagner, the man who'd spoken to me first and who was currently behind the wheel, had allowed me to text my mother and tell her to come back to the house to watch the animals and babysit the chicken in the oven...and to be there when Noah showed up, since I didn't want to push my luck by asking to send a second text, this one to my boyfriend. Even with all that handled, I couldn't help fretting.

Had the charm not worked? Had the Dunstable police, against all odds, somehow found a scrap of evidence to show I'd been upstairs and therefore must have been responsible for all the destruction in Milton Keyes's bedroom? Or had Adelaide Hanford decided to rat me out after all?

I supposed I'd find out soon enough.

Like the cruiser, the police station in Dunstable was shiny and clean and fairly new. Officer Wagner and his partner escorted me into Chief Stanton's office and left.

The police chief didn't seem terribly thrilled to see me. "Have a seat, Ms. Hughes."

I sat down on the chair that faced his desk. Unlike all the stereotypical police chiefs' desks I'd seen in movies or on television, this one was immaculate, with not even a pen out of place. No pieces of paper, no stacks of case files. I couldn't tell whether he really was that neat or whether there just wasn't a lot going on in quiet little Dunstable.

Hoping I looked utterly unassuming and not at all like the sort of person who would ransack a dead man's bedroom, I said, "Can I ask what this is about?"

One brow lifted ever so slightly. "I think you know, Ms. Hughes. Adelaide Hanford got in touch with us after she saw what you did to her brother's room."

"I didn't do anything to her brother's room," I responded at once, which was only the truth. After all, the destruction had occurred long before I got there.

Chief Stanton didn't reply for a moment. His

cool eyes were studying my face, looking for the lie there. However, since my previous reply had been true, I hoped he wouldn't find anything of note.

"Right," he said, tone disbelieving. "Because you were only in the house to get some dog food."

"I was," I said. "Why does that sound so strange?"

He leaned back in his chair. I realized then it was well past six o'clock, and I kind of doubted he generally worked this late. Better not to bring that up, though; I had a feeling that commenting about him missing dinner because of a fishing expedition wouldn't earn me many brownie points.

"Ms. Hughes, most people wouldn't make a round trip of nearly a hundred miles to get dog food."

"Well," I said mildly. "I'm not most people. I foster animals. Chihuahuas have very delicate constitutions, and if you change their food on them abruptly, they can have stomach problems. The only way to find out what kind of food Lexi eats was to get it from her house. Like I told Ms. Hanford, I didn't break in. The door was unlocked."

"So it was," Chief Stanton said, now looking irritated. I had to guess he'd already grilled his deputies to try to find out who had been careless enough to leave the back door unlocked, to no avail. And because I'd used magic to get in, it wasn't as if he'd be able to find evidence of lock-picking or anything close to it. "Still, while it wasn't breaking and entering, it was trespassing."

"I know," I responded, since there wasn't much point in trying to deny I'd been inside the house. "And I would never have done something like that if I weren't trying to take care of Lexi. Bad enough that she lost her master so suddenly and horribly. I didn't want to make her sick with unfamiliar dog food on top of that."

The whole time I was talking, I did my best to hold the police chief's gaze and convince him of my sincerity. However, it probably didn't help that while I spoke, an unbidden image of Lexi gobbling down bits of pepperoni and sausage from Noah's and my pizza the other night kept flickering in my mind.

Delicate stomach?

Not so much.

However, it seemed that Chief Stanton didn't own a chihuahua and didn't know much about them, because he didn't try to contradict my statements about the little dogs' delicate constitutions.

"So, you're telling me you didn't go upstairs."

"No," I answered at once, all the while praying that my falsely innocent expression hadn't shifted a single bit. "I went into the kitchen and looked in the pantry and the cupboards, but I couldn't find Lexi's food anywhere."

"That's because Mr. Keyes kept it in the laundry room," Chief Stanton said.

I allowed myself a single silent thank-you to the universe for that piece of information. It was the same thing I'd speculated about to Adelaide Hanford, but until this moment, I hadn't known whether it was true.

"Oh, I didn't think to look there," I told him, and his lip curled.

"Good thing. You already poked around enough as it was." He paused there and fixed me with a narrow-eyed look that made me want to squirm in my chair, although I managed to hold on and gaze back at him as innocently as I could. "Are you willing to swear in a court of law that you didn't go upstairs?"

Somehow, I managed to hold his stare...and even refrained from making a betraying swallow. "Are you charging me with something, Chief Stanton?"

He didn't blink. "No. Unfortunately, we couldn't find any evidence that you'd been anywhere near Mr. Keyes's bedroom—the only fingerprints we were able to locate were his—or that the back door lock was tampered with in any way. Lacking any real proof, I can't really bring you in front of a judge."

Relief blossomed in me, although I did my best

to remain impassive. "Then why have me come here?"

"Because I wanted to talk to you in person. I wanted to see if you looked guilty."

Again, I held myself still, even as I wondered if maybe I'd missed out on a career as an award-winning actress somewhere along the way. "I just wanted to help Lexi. That's all."

For the first time, the grim set of his features relaxed slightly. "I believe you about that, Ms. Hughes. And I suppose I should thank you for taking the dog. Ms. Hanford told me she couldn't bring Lexi home because her daughter is deathly allergic."

Nice story, but I didn't believe it for a second. No, Adelaide had just wanted to offer a convincing excuse for her heartlessness, and it looked like Chief Stanton had bought the whole thing.

Somehow, I didn't think he was as good a judge of human nature as he thought he was.

"Does this mean I'm free to go?" I asked, and he scowled.

"Yes," he replied, then added before I could react, "Just make sure I don't see you around here anytime soon."

No problem with that. Since Milton Keyes' house seemed like a dead end at this point, there wasn't any reason for me to return to Dunstable.

And thank God for that.

But....

"Will your deputies take me home, or do I need to call a friend for a ride?"

His scowl deepened. "They'll take you back. Have a good evening."

I had no idea whether that was the way these things were normally handled or whether he was feeling sheepish for dragging me in here on extremely skimpy pretenses. Either way, I wouldn't have to ask my mother or Noah or someone else to give me a ride home, for which I was grateful.

All the same, I had a feeling it was going to be an awkward drive back to Salem.

When I got home, it was to find both my mother and Noah there, which I hadn't been expecting. After she gave me a relieved hug and asked me if I was okay, I shot her a questioning look.

"Well, dinner was in the oven," she said. "And I thought it would be better if we both waited here for you. There are leftovers in the fridge—let me get you a plate."

She got up from the couch and hurried into the kitchen, while Noah's worried blue eyes met mine.

"Are you okay?"

"I am now," I said truthfully. Just being there with him—and having Milo and Lexi nearby, tails wagging, relief clear in every line of their bodies—made me feel about a thousand percent better. "Chief Stanton just wanted to talk to me. I guess someone went upstairs in Milton Keyes' house and really trashed the place, and since I was the one who found the body...."

If anything, the frown tugging at Noah's brows only deepened. "But the police must have gone upstairs between now and then. Why would they think you had anything to do with it?"

Because of course I hadn't told Noah about my foray to the place earlier today. No, I'd thought I could skip over that part...and I still needed to somehow get around it. Telling him I'd gone over there to find Lexi's food wouldn't fly because he knew I'd already bought some for her here in Salem.

I shrugged. "Grasping at straws, I guess. There wasn't any sign of forced entry and I guess it doesn't look like anything was taken. I sort of have the feeling that Chief Stanton is out of his element with this one."

Noah reached out and wrapped his fingers around mine, warm and strong and exactly what I needed right then. "Well, I guess I can see that. I doubt they get too many crimes like this in Dunstable. Still, he shouldn't be dragging innocent people in for questioning just because he doesn't have a clue what to do next."

"I know," I replied. "But the important thing is that I'm exonerated, so we can move on." I glanced down at Lexi, who still stood there, tail wagging. While I hated to lie to Noah, I knew I couldn't say I'd used magic to enter Milton Keyes' house and had been accosted by his sister there. Well, a tiny little fib wouldn't hurt anyone, and I knew he'd be happy to know that Lexi was now a permanent part of the household. "I heard from Adelaide Hanford this afternoon. She told me she can't take Lexi because her daughter is allergic, so it looks like the dog is staying here with me."

At once, Noah's face lit up, and although Lexi's tail continued to wag, I could tell she looked puzzled as well. To my relief, though, she didn't even try to say something but instead went dancing over to the dining room table, where my mother had just set down my plate of reheated leftovers.

"Go ahead and eat," Noah told me. "You must be starving."

I was. And even though it would feel strange to sit down and eat when no one else was, I knew I needed to get some food in my system.

So I pulled out a chair from the dining room

table, and my mother and Noah followed suit. I had to admit the chicken and roasted potatoes were great, probably a lot better than they would have been if I'd made them myself. Of course, Milo and Lexi were happy, because I paused to give them a little morsel now and then, even though I had a feeling they'd already gotten their share of treats while my boyfriend and mother were eating dinner earlier.

Once I'd slowed down a little—and had some wine, since they had thoughtfully left about half the bottle for me—Noah ventured, "I wonder why anyone would do that to Milton Keyes's house?"

I wouldn't allow myself to look at my mother, since the two of us knew very well why someone would think it a good idea to rummage through his things. "Well, he owned an antique store and had a lot of expensive furniture. Maybe some thieves got word that the house was empty and decided to take a look to see if he had any valuable watches or jewelry, things like that."

My suggestion must have seemed plausible to Noah, because he nodded, saying, "I can see that happening. But how did they get in? You said there wasn't any sign of a break-in."

Right. I wasn't in the habit of telling lies, and now I could see why. Having to keep them straight could get pretty exhausting.

"It sounds like one of the investigators didn't

lock the back door properly," I said, and helped myself to another bite of roasted potato. "At least, that's what I think. Otherwise, the police would have been able to tell that either the front or the back door was forced open. I suppose it's up to them—and maybe Milton's sister—to find out if anything is actually missing or whether the thieves trashed the place after they realized there wasn't anything worth taking."

"Or at least was easily portable," my mother put in, and Noah sent her a questioning look. She offered him a small smile, adding, "That is, it sounds as if most of the furniture was fairly valuable, but a credenza isn't exactly the kind of thing you can sneak out of a house in your back pocket."

That comment made him chuckle a little, which I guessed had been its exact intent. The conversation moved on from there, with Noah telling me I should bring Lexi in for a full exam sometime next week after the dust had settled.

"Not that she doesn't look like she's in perfect health," he added. "But when she was at the clinic, I was mostly checking to see if she was microchipped or had any obvious signs of trauma. It couldn't hurt to look her over a little more thoroughly...and maybe by then you'll have gotten some vet records from Milton's sister, or at least learned who Lexi's vet was."

The thought of Adelaide Hanford voluntarily

handing over the dog's vet records made me want to laugh. Then again, my asking for the information would seem like a tacit understanding that Lexi was now officially mine, so maybe Adelaide would be happy enough to comply if she thought it meant she'd never have to hear from me again.

"I'll try asking her tomorrow or the next day," I said, which I hoped would let Noah know that I'd take care of the issue in my own time. Honestly, Lexi really didn't seem as if she needed an exam, but I knew he was just trying to be thorough, especially since she was joining a household where there was already another dog.

Noah seemed content with my reply, though, which was one of the things I loved about him. He never pushed, was always willing to listen to my side of things. Most people would say that was how adults were supposed to handle their personal lives, but after a couple of the guys I'd dated in recent history, his attitude was definitely a breath of fresh air.

By that point, I'd eaten as much as I wanted to, and the conversation had begun to wind down. My mother seemed to realize it was time to get going, so she wished us both a good night and told me she'd see me tomorrow when I dropped off the dogs. That comment made Noah raise an eyebrow, but to my relief, he didn't ask any questions until she was safely out the door.

"You're having your mother watch Lexi and Milo?" he said. "I thought it seemed like they got on just fine here by themselves."

"They do," I replied. "But I really need to get back into the shop tomorrow, and since this whole murder and dognapping thing isn't anywhere close to being resolved, I thought it would be better if they weren't left alone."

His expression sobered. "I suppose I can see that. Your mom's house has a fenced yard?"

I wanted to smile at how concerned he was for Lexi's welfare. True, Milo was involved here, too, but Noah knew Milo pretty well and understood he wasn't the kind of dog to stray, while Lexi was still something of an unknown quantity.

"Completely fenced," I assured him. "And because my mom's home all day, she can let them in and out as needed."

Not to say that she didn't work; she had quite the online presence as a sort of lifestyle guru for people who were into "cottagecore," which I still hadn't quite figured out. But she had thousands and thousands of followers on all the various social media platforms and got hefty checks from YouTube and lots of lucrative endorsements for her Instagram and TikTok accounts, and was always making new videos and posts and that kind of stuff. I had to admit, it was kind of funny she earned her money that way when I only went on social media when I absolutely couldn't avoid it any longer.

However, my mother's work definitely allowed her to be around to keep an eye on the dogs, which I knew was the important thing.

"Then it sounds like it's the perfect situation for them," Noah said. "And hopefully, the Dunstable P.D. will be able to track down the killer soon, and things can go back to normal."

I had my doubts as to the police department's ability to find such a cold-blooded murderer, but I kept them to myself. Whoever we were dealing with here, it seemed to me they were more than capable of lying low and evading notice, which meant it was probably up to me—with, I hoped, some assistance from my coven members—to figure out who really had killed Milton Keyes, and why.

And also, with a little luck, to discover where that grimoire had gone. It wasn't exactly the sort of thing you'd want just floating around out there.

"Back to normal sounds good," I said, and Noah bent and gave me a warm, reassuring, and entirely welcome kiss.

His voice came to my ear. "Do you think Lexi would mind if I stayed over? My first surgery tomorrow isn't until nine."

I glanced over at the dog, who'd settled herself on the rug but was still watching us through half-closed sleepy eyes. Sooner or later, she'd need to understand that Noah and I had a physical relationship, and since she seemed pretty mellow right now, I couldn't think of a better time.

"No," I said firmly. "I'm sure she won't mind."

Chapter 11

Nosing Around

"Are you going to marry him?" Lexi asked me the next morning after Noah had left for work, and I nearly choked on my mouthful of toothpaste.

Somehow, I managed to keep on brushing, then spat out the toothpaste, rinsed my mouth, and said, "Why in the world would you ask me that?"

Her little head tilted past the bathroom door and toward the bedroom. "Isn't that what's supposed to happen when people do what you did last night?"

Oh, boy. Noah and I had come upstairs and climbed into bed the evening before, but as far as I could tell, Milo had managed to keep Lexi down in the living room while certain events were going on. However, we hadn't shut the door, so I assumed a few key sounds must have drifted down the staircase.

Since the two of us hadn't even exchanged the L-word yet, I knew marriage wasn't on the docket any time soon.

"It happens sometimes," I replied carefully. Then I paused and sent a curious look down at the little dog. Milo had already headed downstairs to get some water, so at least I was alone with Lexi.

It was a horribly personal question, but I had to ask.

"Did Milton ever...you know?"

"Have sex?" Lexi responded.

Luckily, I was done with the toothpaste, so I didn't have to worry about performing a spit-take. All the same, I had to wonder where the dog had gotten her vocabulary when she'd only been talking for the past couple of days.

"Yes," I said, hoping I didn't look too awkward.

"He had a woman over a few times a while ago," Lexi replied. "But then she never came back, so I assumed things didn't work out. Which was fine by me. I didn't like her very much."

Dogs could often be possessive of their humans and not appreciate intrusion by someone they viewed as a rival, so this bit of news didn't surprise me very much. "Do you remember what she looked like?"

Lexi frowned. "She came and went at night,

and I didn't like being in the same room with her, so I never got a good look. She smelled funny, though."

That was an odd bit of information. Milton Keyes had seemed like a fastidious person, and I couldn't really imagine him dating someone with body odor. "Funny how?"

"Just funny. Kind of like how you smelled yesterday when you came in from gathering those herbs in the garden, except not fresh and happy. More like...damp and mildewy. I don't think it was anything Milton would have noticed, though. People aren't very perceptive about that kind of thing."

This last sentence was pronounced with a definite sniff at the end, clearly expressing Lexi's disapproval of humans' substandard olfactory abilities. However, I wasn't too worried about that. What struck me was that the smell the dog had described was the sort of thing you might encounter when someone was creating potions with dark ingredients or casting spells that required the sorts of components that would never go into one of my elixirs.

Had Milton's mystery woman been a witch?

Could she have been *the* witch?

But no, that didn't make much sense, because if Milton had been dating the woman who'd yelled at him in his store, then Lexi would have already commented on that.

Once again, I got the feeling that I was looking at a puzzle with way too many missing pieces.

"You're sure you don't remember anything about what the woman Milton was seeing looked like?" I asked then, knowing I probably sounded a little too desperate. "Nothing at all? Height, hair color?"

"Her hair was dark…I think," Lexi said. "And she was bigger than you."

"Heavier?"

Lexi gave an emphatic shake, one that made the new collar I'd bought her rattle a bit. She still needed tags, but that was something I could take care of this week. When I'd bought the collar, I hadn't known for sure whether the dog would be going to Adelaide or not, so I hadn't bothered with buying a tag as well.

"Not bigger around," the chihuahua explained patiently. "Bigger up and down."

Taller than me…which fit the description of the woman who'd cast the spell of speaking on Lexi in the first place. Now I really wished I'd been able to get a good look at her face during my scrying, rather than only catching a glimpse of her from the side.

Could it be possible that I was dealing with two separate witches here?

Maybe Milton had been dating a witch who practiced dark magic, and then when things went south, she'd stabbed him and stolen his heart. I still thought that sounded like an extreme reaction to a break-up, but then, witches who took the left-hand path weren't always known for their rationality.

That still didn't explain the missing grimoire or the woman who thought Milton had it.

I needed some tea. True, I'd just brushed my teeth, but I figured a nice cup of green tea spiked with ginger wouldn't cause too much of a problem, and clearly, the coffee I'd had with breakfast earlier hadn't been enough to get all my synapses firing.

"Let's go downstairs," I told Lexi. She didn't seem at all put off by the abrupt shift in topic and happily followed me down the staircase and into the kitchen, where Milo was nosing around on the floor, probably looking for any dropped bits of bread or bacon.

His tail wagged at our arrival, and he said, "Are we still going to your mother's today?"

"That's the plan," I replied. Noah had left almost a half hour earlier, but since I didn't need to be at the shop until a little before ten, I had enough time to be leisurely. "You'll like it, I promise. Think of it as a change in scenery."

That suggestion made him brighten a bit. "That's true. It'll be interesting to be in a yard I haven't visited before."

I picked up the kettle from the stove, took it over to the sink, and began filling it with water. "And I already told her what kinds of treats you like, so I think it will be a lot of fun."

Both Milo and Lexi brightened at my comment. They looked toward the dog door, and I said, "I'm sure it's fine to go outside for a bit. I'll just stay in here until you're done."

Glad that they weren't confined to the house, they both scampered outside while I headed to the cupboard and got down the small jar that contained my green tea with ginger. After scooping some into a tea ball and setting it on the counter next to my mug, I waited for the kettle to near a boil, frowning as I considered this latest piece of information Lexi had given me.

Was it possible Milton had been dating a dark witch, or was I just jumping to that conclusion because it tied up the whole mystery in a neat little ball?

Well, as neat as it could be when I had no idea who the witch was or where she lived. And I had a feeling that trying to scry her exact location wouldn't help, because anyone who practiced that kind of magic would make sure she and her home were warded against that sort of enchantment. It seemed likely to me the only reason I'd been able to catch a glimpse of her at all was because I'd seen images of her when she was out in the world, not at her house. Even then, I'd only been granted a quick sideways glimpse and nothing more.

I blew out a sigh as the water in the kettle began to bubble, then turned off the gas. None of this was making much sense.

One thing seemed clear enough to me, though.

I was very, very glad the two dogs wouldn't be staying at home alone.

The drop-off went smoothly enough. I handed over the plastic bags of dog food I'd packed earlier to my mother and told her I'd call at lunch to see how everything was going.

"It'll be fine," she assured me, smiling as the dogs wandered around the living room, sniffing everything in sight. "We'll have a nice, cozy time together, and then you can pick them up this afternoon."

I hoped so. But no suspicious cars had followed me, and I'd cast an enchantment of my own this morning, one I hoped would make it more difficult for any unfriendly eyes to spy on what I was up to. It was all I could do, even as I was nagged by the feeling that I should have taken more preventive measures.

Summoning an answering smile, I said, "Sounds good. I'll call around twelve-thirty or so, depending on when I can take a break." I looked over at Milo and Lexi and added, "And you two be good."

"Aren't we always?" Milo responded, and I could only shake my head, smiling despite myself.

The two of them had only been together for a couple of days, but I could tell they were already partners in crime.

With that handled, I went ahead to the shop, pulling into my parking space behind the building at around ten before the hour. No sign of Sage's Nissan Leaf yet, but she often didn't get to work until a few minutes before we were supposed to open, since it was technically my job to prep the cash register and unlock the door.

Even though everything about my drive to work had seemed relentlessly normal, I couldn't help sending a brief wary glance around the shop as I stepped inside and turned off the alarm, then flicked on the lights. I didn't see any lurking witches or a single thing out of place, telling me Sage must have had plenty of time yesterday to tidy things up before she left.

So far, so good.

I went ahead and opened the cash register and the front door. Just as I was getting the little bag of money from yesterday's transactions out of the safe in the storeroom, Sage appeared. She was nearly seven years younger than I, with fawn-brown hair and greenish eyes, and as usual was dressed casually, in jeans and a long-sleeved knit top. I didn't have any kind of a dress code at Full Moon Apothecary and usually wore a similar kind of outfit. Mine definitely wasn't one of those Salem shops where the staff was expected to dress up in witchy-looking clothes...even though both its employees actually were witches.

"How's everything with the dogs?" she asked. While I hadn't given Sage a lot of details, I had to assume her mother, Izzy Halloran, had talked to my mother—and maybe Grace Bowersby—at some point and gotten the skinny about my current investigation.

"They're fine," I said. "They're at my mom's today. It's probably an unnecessary precaution, but I just wanted to make sure they were safe."

"I think it's a good idea," Sage replied. "The stuff my mother told me about this latest murder made it sound pretty bad."

"Oh, it is," I said. "Luckily, I don't think it has much to do with us in Salem, except for Lexi being abandoned here, so I'm pretty sure we don't have anything to worry about."

That might have been a little too optimistic an opinion of the situation, but I didn't want to freak Sage out too much. Besides, so far I hadn't seen a single shred of evidence to show that the witch who'd killed Milton Keyes was anywhere nearby. It really did seem as if she'd done her dirty work in Dunstable and then had retreated to whatever lair she called home.

I had to stop the conversation there because our first customers came in, a man and wife I guessed were tourists, since they didn't look familiar to me and I knew all our local regulars. The couple seemed more interested in looking around than actually buying something, and after a few minutes, they headed out without exchanging a single word with us beyond my initial, "Just let me know if you have a question about anything."

Obviously, they didn't, but we had a fairly steady flow of customers after that, more than I would have expected on a Wednesday morning. Because of the influx of patrons, I didn't have a chance to grab lunch until nearly one o'clock, when I finally escaped to the break room with the sandwich Sage had brought me so I could steal a few minutes to myself and check in with my mother. She hated texts, which meant I had to call.

"How are the dogs?" I asked.

"They're fine," she said. I couldn't see her, but I guessed she was smiling as she spoke. "They had their lunch about forty-five minutes ago and then went to play in the yard. Now they're crashed on the sofa."

About what I'd expected, but I was still glad to

hear the dogs were having a good day. "And no one suspicious around?"

"Of course not," she replied, still sounding amused. "The UPS guy came by a half hour ago and dropped off that new ring light I ordered, but otherwise, everything has been quiet as the grave."

Not a phrase I would have used, considering the current circumstances, but I wasn't going to comment. "That's good to hear. It's been pretty busy here. Nothing out of the ordinary, though."

"I doubt there will be," my mother said. "If nothing else, a strange witch is going to think twice about coming into Salem and doing whatever she wants, considering how big our magical community is here."

She had a point there. Many towns had only one coven each, yet here in Salem, we had three of them, thanks to the city's unique reputation and the much more welcoming attitude toward all things witchy here. True, most of the women who walked the streets wearing black clothes and pointed hats were just playing dress-up—we real witches reserved that sort of garb for special ceremonies—but it was true that the witches who lived in my hometown could join forces if necessary and send a single interloper packing.

"You're probably right," I said. "Still, I'm glad we're being careful."

"Of course," my mother replied. "And I'll keep

watching the dogs for as long as I need to. They're both wonderful creatures."

Yes, they were. My mom was a little handicapped in that she couldn't speak to Milo directly because she didn't have my gift for talking to familiars, but since the spell on Lexi allowed her to talk to anyone who was a witch, she could act as a go-between if necessary.

"Okay," I said. "I'll be by a little after five to get them."

"See you then," she responded sunnily, and that was the end of that.

Afternoon at the shop wasn't quite as busy as the morning, but we still had enough customers that Sage and I didn't have much of a chance to talk. In a way, I was fine with that, just because I didn't want to say anything that might unnerve her any more than she already was. As it was, we locked up promptly at five and went our separate ways, with me taking a detour so I could swing by my mother's house and collect the dogs.

They were both looking pretty chipper, so I knew they'd had a good time. Noah had texted me a few hours earlier to ask if I wanted to bring them to his place and have Thai takeout, so instead of heading home, I drove over to his house and pulled up in the driveway.

Both Milo and Lexi were so well-behaved that I didn't worry about putting leashes on them for the short walk from my car to the front door, although I noticed his across-the-street neighbor giving me the stink-eye for letting them run free.

Well, Mrs. Muzzio had always come across as sort of a busybody to me.

Noah opened the front door in answer to my knock, and at once Lexi rushed inside, wanting to smell everything and get the lay of the land. Milo followed at a more sedate pace, since he'd been here plenty of times before and the house was almost as familiar to him as his own home.

"How was work?" Noah asked as he closed the front door, the corners of his mouth twitching a bit as Lexi roamed around the Persian rug in the living room, sniffing delightedly at every square inch.

"It was fine," I said. "Quiet, which I greatly appreciated."

"I can imagine," he replied with a chuckle, then leaned down so he could give me a quick kiss. "Glass of wine?"

"Please."

We went into the kitchen, where Milo and Lexi followed, looking a little disappointed that there weren't any cooking smells.

"Takeout tonight, kids," I told them, whereupon they seemed to relax slightly.

Still wearing a half smile, Noah got a bottle of rosé out of the fridge and poured a glass for me and then himself. "The usual?" he asked after he'd returned the bottle to the refrigerator and gotten out the menu for the local Thai place, which he kept in a drawer with a bunch of other takeout menus. Yes, all that information was on the internet, but I had to admit it was still easier to look at a printed menu rather than trying to squint at the offerings online on a tiny phone screen.

After everything that had happened over the past twenty-four hours, I really wasn't in the mood to be adventurous. "The usual would be great."

He dug his phone out of his pocket and placed our regular order for sweet and sour chicken, pad Thai, wontons, and fried rice...and then took a second look at my face and threw in some mango sticky rice for dessert as well. Yes, I'd had a quiet day at work, but my brain had kept working away at all the contradictory clues that currently crowded it, and I had a feeling I still looked pretty strained.

For about the millionth time, I wished Noah knew all about my witchy side so I could mention Lexi's revelations from this morning and ask whether he thought it was possible that the woman Milton had been seeing a few months ago was the same one who'd murdered the man in cold blood. But even though we were close, and even though I knew I cared about him more than I'd ever cared about anyone else, I still couldn't quite bring myself to take that step.

We headed out to the living room to wait for the takeout to arrive. After Noah and I had sat down—and Lexi and Milo had positioned themselves near the front door so they could let us know the second the Uber Eats driver was coming up the walk—he said, "I know we talked about next week to have me look at Lexi, but one of my clients just canceled their Friday morning appointment because they had to go out of town for a family emergency. Do you think you could bring her in then?"

I'd been in the middle of sipping my rosé when Noah asked the question, so I had to swallow before I could respond. "Maybe," I said slowly. "I really think I need to try getting in touch with Adelaide Hanford first to see if she has access to any of Lexi's vet records. If she doesn't...or if she just won't hand them over...then sure, it's probably a good idea for you to look at the dog. I just don't want to have her go through an exam now if she just had one last month or something."

And true, I could have asked Lexi about her vet visits, but dogs didn't have the same time sense as humans—although familiars tended to be better about those sorts of things—and I doubted whether she'd be able to give me anything close to an exact date, or even tell me that she'd been to the vet in the past few months. It seemed better to get more concrete information from Adelaide, despite how difficult she was to deal with.

For a second or two, I'd been worried that maybe Noah would be offended by my insinuation that one of his exams was something that needed to be "gotten through." However, he only gave an understanding nod as he said, "That makes sense. Just don't be too surprised if Ms. Hanford isn't very cooperative."

Because I'd already mentally prepared myself for that eventuality, I could only smile. "Oh, don't worry," I said. "At this point, I wouldn't be surprised by much of anything...."

Chapter 12

Foreign Objects

Because Noah had an early surgery Thursday morning, I didn't stay too late at his house, just long enough to share our dinner of takeout Thai—while feeding some choice morsels to the dogs, naturally—before heading home. When we got there, it was barely nine o'clock, which gave me some time to mentally prepare myself for the phone call I knew I'd need to make to Adelaide Hanford the next morning.

And do some research. At this point, the only things I really knew about her were that she was divorced, lived in Lowell, and had a daughter. I had no idea what she did for a living, or what her address and phone number were.

Those pieces of information were something I could obtain through the use of a simple spell, but I realized she'd be even more suspicious of me if I suddenly came up with her contact information out of the blue. Better to find it on the Internet if at all possible.

That was why I sat down with my laptop and a glass of water in the living room while Lexi and Milo lay down on the rug in front of the hearth, even though the weather was still too warm to even think about having a fire. Still, it was a cozy spot, and a good place to unwind until I was ready for bed.

To my surprise, my search for "Adelaide Hanford" came back almost at once. Apparently, she was a junior partner at a law firm in Lowell, and that meant she had a publicly available phone number, one I could use without rousing any suspicions.

It looked like she did her fair share of litigation, which explained why she'd been so combative when she confronted me the day before. And all right, I'd been snooping around where I shouldn't have, but there wasn't any reason for her to be quite so hostile.

Now all I had to do was hope she wouldn't be in court when I called her firm tomorrow morning. I'd have plenty of time to reach out before I needed to leave for work, even allowing the extra buffer I needed to drop the dogs off at my mother's house on the way in.

I found myself hoping it would turn out that

Lexi had gone to the vet recently so there wouldn't be any need for Noah to give her an exam. It wasn't that I didn't trust him to be gentle and kind, but still, that kind of examination would be intrusive no matter how solicitous he was during the process, and I would much prefer to skip the whole thing.

However, I'd told him I'd allow him to look her over, so I couldn't back out now. All I could do was cross my fingers that Lexi's shots had all been updated a few weeks before and we could just blow past the whole thing.

She'd been through enough already.

Adelaide Hanford was in the office when I called around nine-thirty...and didn't seem too happy to hear from me.

"What do you want now?" she snapped after I greeted her.

Count to three, I told myself. Biting back at her wouldn't earn me any points, that was for sure.

"I was hoping you might know when Lexi went to the vet last," I replied, marveling a little at how unruffled I sounded. It sure felt as if I'd upped my game these past few months when it came to dealing with difficult people. "Or at least if you have any idea where you might be able to access her vet records, or even which veterinarian your brother took her to."

A sound came through my phone's speaker that I thought was an exasperated sigh. "I have absolutely no idea," she said. "It wasn't anything I needed to know, and Milton never brought it up in conversation. Why do you need that information now? The dog always seemed perfectly healthy to me."

Somehow I got the impression Adelaide was thinking, *Too healthy,* although even she apparently realized saying that kind of thing aloud was going way too far.

"Because a friend of mine is a vet here in Salem, and he thought it might be a good idea to look her over if she hadn't seen a vet recently," I replied. "But obviously, we don't want to give her another round of shots if she's gotten them within the past year."

"I don't know," Adelaide said. "The only thing I do know is that the dog is three and a half, so if Milton took her every year, then she should need some coming up soon."

Not what I'd wanted to hear, but better than nothing. At least the woman knew the age of the dog she disliked so much. I'd guessed that Lexi was fairly young, but if she was a little past three, then she had a good long life ahead of her, especially since I knew that small dogs tended to live longer than large ones.

"Okay," I said, still maintaining the falsely cheerful voice I'd assumed to keep myself from snapping right back at Milton's prickly sister, "well, that at least gives me something to go on. I won't take up any more of your time."

"Good," she returned, and hung up. At least, I assumed she had an actual landline to hang up, since I was calling her at her number at the law office.

I stuffed my phone in my purse and allowed myself a mental growl now that I was no longer talking to the woman. It wasn't like me to allow such an uncharitable thought to pass through my mind, but right then I could see why she was divorced.

Who in the world would want to live with that?

At some point, I'd need to text Noah to let him know systems were go for Lexi's exam, but since he'd told me he had back-to-back surgeries this morning, I figured I could let it go for now. Better to get the dogs packed up and off to my mother's, and then I could get in touch with Noah when I had an open spot in my day.

But even though I knew it was best for the dog to have a professional really look her over, I couldn't help thinking all of this was a very bad idea.

That sense of foreboding continued to hang over me, even though everything at the store that day was fairly mellow and we had just enough customers to keep us busy without things getting too crazy. We had a small break at eleven that gave me some time to send a text to Noah about Lexi's exam, which was set for ten o'clock Friday morning. I'd have to leave work and then come back once he was finished, but I hoped the whole process wouldn't take much more than a half hour.

"It's fine," Sage assured me when I told her I'd have to pop out for a bit the next morning. Her greenish eyes danced as she added, "It's not like you're leaving me alone on Memorial Day weekend or anything."

Even though I knew she was joking, I couldn't help giving a mental wince. Last May, I'd had to leave my assistant alone in the shop during that busy holiday when I was trying to track down the man who'd murdered Milo's mistress. The situation had been pretty much unavoidable, but I still felt bad about it.

"No, nothing like that," I replied, knowing I'd already apologized enough times that to keep doing so now would just sound silly. "And if it's going to take anything more than a half hour, I'll let you know."

She nodded, but then a group of tourists came in and we had to abandon our conversation so we could show them where the arthritis and insomnia tinctures were located, and where we also kept packets of herbal tea. The activity distracted us long enough that it didn't seem necessary to revisit our earlier topic, so I just let it go.

I'd take Lexi to have Noah look at her, it would be entirely routine, and I'd be back at work before anyone even noticed I'd been missing.

He came over that night and we ordered takeout again, this time tacos from the Spitfire Grill. Lexi was very interested in begging for pieces of meat from my "vampiro" taco, to the point where I had to tell her to stop because I wouldn't be left with any filling to eat at the rate she was going. It was a quiet, comfortable night, though, with no surprise raids from the Dunstable P.D. or strange witches popping up on my doorstep or cease-and-desist letters coming from Adelaide Hanford telling me I needed to leave her alone.

No, we ate tacos and each had a beer for a change of pace, then watched TV with the dogs once again snuggling on the sofa with us, Milo's head on my knees and Lexi curled into a little ball in Noah's lap. I couldn't help thinking again how wonderful it was for all of us to be here like this, and how good it was to have those fun, furry critters to keep Noah and me company. Even though the circumstances surrounding the way she'd come to be with us had been awful, it still somehow felt as if the universe had always intended her to be part of our impromptu family.

As peaceful as the situation was, though, I couldn't help thinking there had to be another shoe somewhere that was just waiting to drop, that it didn't feel right not to be poking and prodding at the mystery, trying to figure out who had killed Milton and put that spell on Lexi. True, I really didn't have any new evidence to work with, but shouldn't I have been out somewhere trying to find it?

Because I knew I'd never be able to rest completely easy as long as I didn't know for sure if someone was going to come after the little dog I'd adopted. There had to be a darn good reason why an unknown witch had made Lexi speak, even if I still had no idea why.

Luckily, it didn't seem as if Noah noticed any of my inner turmoil as we sat on the couch and watched *Milo and Otis,* a movie our own Milo loved because of hearing his name mentioned over and over during the film. And when we went upstairs afterward, Noah seemed to realize I was only in the mood to snuggle that night, because he drew me close and kissed me and nothing more. Both Milo and Lexi were curled up at the foot of the bed, a definite block to those sorts of activities, but I always could have shooed them out if I'd been feeling frisky.

As it was, I could only be happy that I was able to fall asleep in his arms.

Although we'd be seeing each other at ten, Noah still needed to be at the clinic by eight. I got up with him and made toast and eggs and coffee, then stayed down in the kitchen with the dogs while he went upstairs to shower.

"I like it when he stays over," Milo said, and I smiled.

"Me too. But it's also fun to go to his house."

Lexi tilted her head at me. "I like his house," she announced. "But I like this house better."

"You do?" I replied, amused. While I was glad to hear my home had her approval, I had to admit that on paper, his was nicer—bigger and more recently remodeled, with a much more manicured backyard.

True, I owned my house while Noah was only renting his, but Lexi didn't know that.

"Yes," the little dog said, her tone emphatic. "Your yard is bigger, and there's just something about this house. It's...comfy."

Well, I had to admit it was the kind of place where most people felt at ease, partly because the old house had its own charm thanks to its hundred-plus years, and partly because, while I tried to keep things tidy, the furniture was a well-worn, mismatched jumble that didn't put on any airs. It was the sort of house where you knew you wouldn't get in trouble for putting your feet on the couch.

"I'm glad you think it's comfy," I told her. "We definitely don't stand on ceremony here, Milo, do we?"

His tail wagged. "Nope," he said cheerfully. "It's a friendly house."

Lexi, on the other hand, seemed to turn thoughtful. "Is it all right for me to think that, though? I don't want to sound like I'm disloyal to Milton. It's just...he wouldn't let me get on the sofa or sleep on his bed, and you let me do both those things. Yes, he made sure I had beds in almost all the rooms in our house, but it's still not the same."

No, it wouldn't be. I'd long ago given up worrying about fur everywhere or toenail scratches on my worn leather couch, which was why my house had such a lived-in look.

However, since I could tell Lexi was worried that she'd said the wrong thing, I bent down and scratched her behind her wispy ears, delicate as butterfly wings.

"You're not disloyal," I told her. "I know you loved Milton very much, and I know you were happy living in his house. But if there are things here you like better or make you more comfortable, there's nothing wrong with acknowledging that."

She gave a little shake, her way of letting me know she was absorbing what I'd said, even if she still wasn't quite sure of exactly how she felt about the situation. We had to stop there, though, because I could hear Noah's steps coming down the staircase. Yes, people talked to their dogs all the time, but in most cases, it still didn't sound as if they were holding a real conversation.

He came into the kitchen and gave me a quick kiss. "I'll see you at ten," he said.

"See you then," I replied, and after giving each of the dogs a quick pat and a ruffle of the ears, he headed out the side door.

"I still think you should get married," Lexi announced.

About all I could do was roll my eyes.

I'd told my mother about Lexi's appointment, so she knew I would be dropping Milo off on his own and then would bring the chihuahua by after we were done at Noah's clinic. About all I had time for was a quick hello after she opened the door, and then it was back in my SUV, where Lexi had been waiting on the front seat.

We were running just the teensiest bit late, but I resisted the urge to goose the gas pedal. Noah wouldn't mind if we were five minutes or so behind schedule, although I would have texted him if the gap was going to be any bigger than that.

Someone was backing out of the choice spot near the front walkway when we pulled into the parking lot, so I waited until they had cleared the space and could claim it as my own.

"Wait there," I told Lexi. "I'll come around and put your leash on from the passenger side."

She nodded, looking resigned. I'd spoiled her by not using the leash very much since she joined my household, but they had strict rules about that sort of thing at Noah's clinic, and I wasn't about to try to claim privilege just because I was dating the owner.

I went to the passenger door, opened it, and then clipped on Lexi's leash and let her jump out. She was a very nimble dog, so it wasn't any problem for her to get down to the ground on her own, even though it was a pretty big distance for a dog her size.

No one was in the waiting room when we walked in; I knew Noah tried to space out his appointments as much as he could to avoid any dust-ups between dogs and other animals who might not have been properly socialized. Behind the front desk, Courtney smiled at me and said, "He's waiting for you, Charity. Exam room two."

"Thanks," I replied, smiling at her in return before I led Lexi down the hallway where the examination spaces were located. Number two was almost immediately on my left, and I peered in to see Noah already waiting for us there.

"Hey," he said, and immediately Lexi trotted over toward him, feathery tail swishing against the faux wood tile floor. He bent and petted her, and said, "Okay if I pick you up?"

He spoke directly to her because that was how he treated all his patients, not because he thought she could actually understand every word he was saying. But she gave him a doggy little smile anyway, and he bent and lifted her onto the exam table.

"What are you expecting to find?" I asked as I came over so I could stroke her back and unclip her leash.

"Probably nothing," he said easily. "I can tell she was well taken care of by her former owner. But

I'll check her teeth and look for any signs of ticks, that sort of thing."

"I do not have ticks," Lexi declared.

Of course, I understood exactly what she'd said, but to Noah, it probably sounded like a tiny sneeze. He ruffled her ears and said, "This won't take very long, Lexi. You've been a very good dog."

She preened a little, which I assumed was what he'd hoped she would do. After unclipping the penlight from the pocket of his lab coat—more than once, I'd thought the coat made him look even hotter, if that was possible—he shone it into her ears and opened her tiny mouth so he could look inside.

"Her teeth are in great shape," he said. "It's pretty obvious she had them cleaned regularly. And her ears are clean, too."

"Well, of course," I replied. "I could already tell that Milton Keyes took really good care of her."

Most men probably would have shot me a pained glance at that not-so-subtle "I told you so." Noah, on the other hand, continued with his inspection, running his hands over Lexi's chest and forelegs, then feeling her back and stomach.

When he got to her hind legs, though, his brows drew together in a sudden, startled frown.

"What's the matter?" I asked, fear darting through me. Was it possible something really was wrong with the dog despite all her outward appearances of good health?

"I don't know," Noah replied. "I can feel a lump in her left haunch."

"Like a tumor?" I said.

Lexi's dark eyes flared wider with worry, and at once Noah reached over to give her a reassuring pat on the head.

"I'm not sure," he said. "It feels...strange...for lack of a better word. Almost angular."

As far as I knew, tumors didn't have sharp angles. Luckily, though, it didn't seem as if Lexi was in any pain or had any idea that anything was wrong with her leg.

What the heck was going on here?

"I'll need to get an X-ray," he went on. "You can carry her in. It'll only take a minute."

Well, at least I wouldn't be left behind to worry about what was going on with my dog. I picked up Lexi, who was now trembling, and stroked her soft little head as I followed Noah into the X-ray room. I'd never been in here before; Milo had never needed this level of care.

"Can you hold her in place?" Noah asked. "You'll need to wear some protection."

"That's fine," I said stoutly, since I knew I would've donned a deep sea diving suit if it would have helped me take care of the newest member of my family.

As I set Lexi down on the table Noah had indicated, he went to a cabinet and got out one of those heavy lead-filled aprons, then handed it over so I could put it on. My dentist's office had mostly dispensed with the things, but clearly, Noah didn't want to take any chances.

The apron was heavy and bulky, but it didn't prevent me from petting Lexi, running my hand over her silky fur so she'd know she was loved and safe, even in a place as unfriendly as an X-ray room. While I kept her still, Noah brought the machine over so he could angle it at her left leg.

Exactly what had he found in there?

"I'm going to take a series of images in short succession," he told me, not realizing that Lexi could also understand every word he said. "Then we'll take a look and see what's going on."

Although a small shudder went through the dog's tiny body, I could tell she was doing her best not to move. Since Noah hadn't told me to move my hand, I assumed he thought it didn't matter if it showed up in the X-ray, since it wasn't covering any of the leg that was his immediate focus.

Not much more than an eye blink, and then he said, "Okay, got it. Give me a minute, and I'll bring the images in so we can take a look at them."

"And I can take off the apron, right?" I asked.

Now he smiled. "Of course. You can lay it on that chair over there."

He used his chin to indicate a metal and vinyl chair in the corner, probably placed there for anxious pet owners who didn't want to be too far away from their precious cats and dogs. I realized then that Courtney or one of the other lab techs should have come in here to help, and that Noah had decided it was probably better to let me stay and assist instead.

As he headed into the room next door, presumably to develop the X-rays, I went ahead and slid off the heavy apron and put it on the chair. Lexi, good dog that she was, remained standing on the exam table. Even she had probably realized it was too high for her to jump down safely.

I went back and patted her head, and gave her a reassuring smile. She looked up at me with the sort of hopeful look that only a dog could manage, one that showed infinite trust in the humans around them.

All I could do was hope that trust wasn't misplaced.

A few minutes later, Noah came back into the room, an X-ray in one hand. "Okay, let's see what we've got here," he said, and went over to the light table on the opposite side of the space.

I picked up Lexi and walked over to him, then stared down at the X-ray.

No...it couldn't be....

"What the heck is that?" Noah said. His brows

had pulled together in probably one of the deepest frowns I'd ever seen him wear. "Is that a *book?*"

Because the object in Lexi's haunch was a chunky rectangle whose proportions definitely looked like a book, even if it was impossible to make out any details at this resolution.

Not just any book, I realized suddenly.

The missing grimoire.

Before I was able to think of how I could possibly respond to Noah's startled question without sounding like a madwoman, a brilliant flash filled the exam room, and, to my horror, the dark-haired witch whose face I'd only partially seen in my visions appeared out of nowhere, her expression one of pure glee.

"So, that's where she hid it," she said, while my body flooded with terrified adrenaline...and Noah wore the expression of a man who wasn't sure whether he was hallucinating or whether someone had slipped some LSD into his morning coffee. As I frantically searched for a spell I could use to protect us—and realized that none of them were going to do us any good right now—the witch looked at him, her mouth curving in a cruel smile. "And I'll use you to get it out. And you," she added, her cold, dark stare moving to me, "aren't going anywhere."

. . .

Chains of air, unseen but tight,
Hold thee fast with all my might.
Let no limb nor thought take flight,
In stillness dwell, by my rite.

I couldn't move. I couldn't do anything except stand there like the world's most useless statue, protests frozen on my lips, as the witch grabbed Lexi in one arm and Noah in the other, and disappeared as quickly as she had come.

Now I'd seen the witch and the grimoire...and couldn't do damn thing about it.

Chapter 13

Calling the Circle

Although it felt like an eternity, the petrification spell only lasted for about five minutes or so. As soon as it wore off, I pulled in a gasp of air and staggered over to the light table, leaning against it until the rubbery sensation in my legs began to finally dissipate.

What the hell was I supposed to do now?

Get it together, I admonished myself. *Freaking out isn't going to help anyone.*

No, it wasn't. I allowed myself to breathe deeply for a moment more, then made myself do some very quick thinking.

Noah and Lexi had vanished. How in the world was I supposed to explain that?

You don't, I thought. *You're going to walk out of here as if nothing happened, then tell Courtney that Noah wanted to keep Lexi for some more tests and that you would be back to pick her up after lunch. All very normal, all very routine.*

Yes, sooner or later, Courtney would figure out that both Noah and the dog had vanished, but I had to do whatever I could to make it look as though I'd had nothing to do with the way they'd apparently disappeared into thin air. After all, how could I? Noah's assistant would have seen me leave alone and get in my car and drive off. There was no reason for her to suspect his inexplicable disappearance had anything to do with me.

And once I made my getaway, I'd drive right over to my mother's house, tell her what had happened, and get the coven working on this. I knew there was no way in the world I could tangle with a witch who possessed those sorts of powers and live to tell the tale.

All right—time for another Oscar-worthy performance.

A few deep breaths...and then a few more, because I needed all the help I could get...I walked out of the X-ray room and closed the door behind me. It had been shut when Noah first brought Lexi and me in there, so I assumed that was standard operating procedure. As I approached the front desk, I essayed what I hoped was a convincing smile as I said, "Hi, Courtney. Noah's keeping Lexi for a few more tests, so I'm going to come back after lunch to get her."

"Oh, okay," Courtney replied. She didn't appear at all surprised by this development, so it seemed the story I'd concocted wasn't that out of the ordinary. "I'll see you then."

"See you then," I echoed, and headed out the front door. Thank God I'd been able to snag that prime parking space when I got here, because right then, I honestly didn't know whether my still shaky legs would have been able to propel me to the other side of the lot.

I climbed into the Discovery, fastened my seatbelt, and pointed the SUV toward my mother's house. She lived a little closer to the clinic than I did, and only about five or six minutes later, I was pulling into her driveway. Frantic fingers undid the seatbelt, and I hurried out of the vehicle so I could run to the front door and knock.

A moment later, my mother opened it. She was smiling...and why shouldn't she be? For all she knew, everything had gone smoothly and I was just stopping by so I could drop off Lexi on my way to work.

But then she seemed to get a good look at my expression, and instantly her smile faded. "What's wrong?"

"We need to talk," I said, and pushed past her into the living room. Milo caught sight of me and his tail began to wag...and then, like my mother, his happy greeting stopped as he really looked at me.

She closed the door. "What happened?"

"The witch hid the grimoire in Lexi's leg. She appeared out of nowhere and kidnapped Noah and the dog."

"*What?*"

I supposed I could forgive my mother for being a bit incredulous. On the surface, the story sounded absolutely crazy, even to someone who was used to dealing with the unexpected.

But I'd been there, and I knew what I'd seen.

I forced myself to take a breath, even though that panicky sensation had blossomed in my gut again, making me feel as if I'd never be able to suck in enough oxygen to truly fill my lungs. "Noah found a lump in Lexi's leg," I explained. "So he took an X-ray. When we looked at it, we could clearly see there was some kind of weird rectangular object in there."

"Like a book," my mother murmured, and I nodded.

"Exactly. We didn't have any time to process what we were seeing, though, because the witch appeared out of nowhere and took Noah and the dog." I stopped there, giving a disbelieving head shake. Even now, the whole situation felt utterly surreal, like something from one of my worst nightmares.

But I had to tell my mother the whole story because I desperately needed her help. The man I loved—and the sweet dog I'd just adopted—had been abducted by someone I knew was capable of the worst violence possible. Yes, the witch had made it sound as if she needed Noah to remove the shrunken grimoire from Lexi, but once that surgery had been accomplished, would she simply shrug and let them go?

Somehow, I doubted it.

My mother came over and gave me a hug, while Milo stood a few feet away, expression and posture utterly disconsolate. I knew he'd gotten close to Lexi, and to lose her like this...not to mention Noah...had to be too much for the dog.

Well, it was too much for me as well, but I needed to stay focused.

"I'll call the coven," my mother said. "You need to text Sage and tell her to close up the shop so she can meet us at Grace's house."

Yes, this was what I needed, for someone else to take charge. I knew how out of my depth I was here. True, I'd faced down the abomination that was Brad Alatorre, but he hadn't been able to truly wield magic, could only turn into a monster and use brute strength to get his way. The woman we were dealing with now was far wilier...and much more dangerous.

"Okay," I said, and scrabbled in my purse so I could get out my phone and message Sage.

Coven emergency. Put the Closed sign on the

door & lock up everything & be @ Grace's house ASAP.

Her response came back almost immediately.

What's going on?

I'll explain @ Grace's. Just do it.

Normally, I would never be that brusque with Sage—or anyone else, really—but we didn't have a moment to waste.

My mother was also on her phone, joining in the group chat we used to organize our ceremonies or any other occasions where we all needed to convene to manage witchy business. A moment later, she looked up, saying, "All right, that's handled. Let's get over to Grace's house."

"I'm going, too," Milo announced, and my mother, who'd taken a step toward the door, stopped suddenly, looking flummoxed. No, she couldn't understand what he'd said, but just his posture signaled that he had no intention of being left out of all this.

Witches brought their familiars to coven meetings all the time, but strictly speaking, Milo wasn't really a familiar. Much closer to one than your ordinary pet, true, and yet I could tell my mother wasn't sure what to do in this wildly unusual situation.

"Yes, you are," I said firmly. "Because this involves all of us. I'll drive—my car's already in the driveway."

My mother didn't seem inclined to argue, only nodded and waited for Milo and me to go out on the front porch so she could lock the door behind us. After that, we all piled into the Land Rover, and I took off toward Grace's house at a speed I knew would have attracted the attention of the Salem P.D. if any of its officers had been anywhere close by.

They weren't, though, and that meant I was able to reach our destination a scant five minutes after we'd left my mother's house. Izzy Halloran, Sage's mother, was just getting out of her car when we pulled up behind her.

"Oh, I hope Noah is all right," she said as soon as we fell in with her and our little group made its way up Grace's front walk.

"I'm sure he is," my mother said, her tone brisk, as if she wasn't about to allow the universe to take him away, not when it looked as if things were getting serious between the two of us. "And we're going to handle this."

When my mother spoke like that, not many people wanted to contradict her, not even the rebellious teen I'd once been. Izzy gave a distracted nod, then opened the door and went inside. When we were gathering like this for an emergency, Grace would always leave the door unlocked so we could go right in and not have to wait for her to let us inside.

Elise Figg was already there; not for the first time, I thought of how strange it felt to have the coven come together and Tonya not be there. She'd always been such a mainstay in our group...and one of its strongest witches. Right then, I couldn't quite hold back a flash of anger at the way she'd betrayed us. Otherwise, we would have been able to rely on her magic to see us through this mess, bringing our coven to the magically charged number of nine and making us that much more powerful.

But her magic was gone, burned out along with her pineal gland, and we were on our own.

All right, not completely on our own. Stella Monroe and her grandmother Valerie came in next, and the tense knot in my stomach eased ever so slightly. Valerie was a powerful witch in her own right, and Stella was no slouch, either.

Together, we might just be able to fix this.

Stella came over to me at once and murmured, "I am so sorry to hear about Noah."

"It's okay," I said, even though it really wasn't. "We'll get him back."

She nodded, jaw set. Even though I knew she had a three-month-old baby at home, she looked darn near perfect, golden-blonde hair pulled back into a sleek ponytail and just a flick of mascara to highlight her clear blue eyes. "Yes, we will."

There wasn't even a flicker of doubt in her

voice, although I supposed she could have been doing her best to sound confident so I wouldn't lose hope. All the same, I found myself cheering up slightly. If I had to go through something so terrible, at least I wouldn't be suffering on my own.

Sage was the last to arrive—no big surprise, since she'd had to close the store and then drive halfway across town to get here. Her worried eyes met mine, but I could tell she was willing to wait and let me explain just what the hell was going on.

"All right," my mother said, after Sage had closed the door behind her and gone to stand next to Izzy. "Now that we're all here, I can bring you up to speed. A dark witch who we think is behind a gruesome murder in Dunstable has kidnapped Noah Jenkins, Charity's boyfriend, along with the dog she just adopted. We believe the witch hid a grimoire in the dog and needs Noah to remove it surgically."

"Miniaturization," Grace murmured, and Elise and Valerie both nodded.

I'd never heard of such a spell, but I'd be the first to admit there was a whole lot about magic I didn't know. Most of the time, I was content to go along in my lane and not do a lot of exploration unless circumstances absolutely demanded it.

Well, they sure seemed to be demanding it now.

"What can you tell us about this witch?" Elise

asked then. "Were you able to get a good look at her?"

"It happened really fast," I said. "But I'd also seen her in a couple of scrying visions, so this last glimpse helped me fill in some of the gaps. She looks like she might be in her early forties, with long, dark brown hair she wears pulled back in a silver clasp. Kind of sharp-featured but not bad-looking."

Except when she wore that horrible gloating smile, but I had to believe she didn't look like that all the time. Even the most powerful of dark witches still had to mingle with mundane society from time to time, had to pick up groceries or get her car repaired or whatever. We'd all learned to blend in as best we could.

Surprisingly, Elise gave a knowing nod. "She sounds like one of the Richter twins."

"Twins?" I blurted.

Like dealing with one evil witch wasn't bad enough?

The corners of Elise's mouth quirked. "Yes, twins," she replied. "But don't worry. They can't stand each other, so I have a feeling we're dealing with Larissa here, not her sister Melissa. Larissa is the one who likes to walk on the dark side, so to speak."

"And how do you know this?" my mother asked.

Elise sent her one of her keen, gray-eyed glances, the one that seemed to say my mother of all people should have known the answer to that question. However, her tone was mild enough as she replied, "Those of us who dabble in the left-hand path get to know one another, especially the witches who are located relatively nearby. The Richter twins live in Lowell. From what I've heard, their mother recently passed on, and they've been bickering over her inheritance ever since."

That revelation made me give a small interior shudder. Mundane people behaved badly enough when it came to dividing up estates. I didn't even want to think what might happen if a couple of witches started feuding about who got the house or the Persian rugs or whatever.

Or the grimoire, I realized suddenly. What if it had been part of the Richter sisters' maternal estate, and they'd fought over that as well?

I asked as much, and Elise nodded. "I could definitely see that happening, even though Melissa Richter wouldn't have much use for that sort of thing. But it's possible she took the grimoire and hid it in Lexi, thinking her sister would never be able to find it there."

"But why would she even think of using the dog?" Sage asked. Her expression was a study of confusion, and I could sympathize. Once again, I got the feeling that none of this made much sense.

And then it clicked, my brain finally grabbing onto the last piece of the puzzle without knowing exactly how it had managed to find it. "Because Melissa was the one who dated Milton Keyes for a while," I said. "The relationship didn't work out, but she must have thought that hiding the grimoire in such a way would safely keep it away from her sister."

Obviously, her ploy hadn't worked. Still, I thought I understood why Melissa had taken Lexi and dropped her off in Salem. She must have hoped the dog would come to me, and that I—and my coven—would be strong enough to protect her until she could safely retrieve the grimoire.

Well, that sure hadn't happened. Now Larissa had both Noah and the dog, and the ticking of the clock on Grace's mantel only served to tell me how quickly time was passing.

"Do you know where they live?" I asked Elise.

"Only that they're in Lowell."

"It's a start," my mother said briskly. "I think it's time to head downstairs and see if we can find out where Larissa Richter has taken Noah."

Everyone murmured their agreement, and we all made our way down the basement steps and into the ceremonial space Grace had created beneath her house. The place was painted a deep green, and she picked up a remote to turn on all the flameless candles that sat in sconces on the walls and on top of the long table set up against the far side of the room.

Without speaking, we formed a circle, our hands finding one another's. I stood with my mother on one side and Elise Figg on the other, and their fingers felt warm and strong against my cold ones.

This had to work. It just had to.

Valerie spoke then. Next to Elise and my mother, she was definitely the strongest of the witches present, and the oldest. It made sense for her to lead us in this spell, the one that would take us to Noah and Lexi.

In Lowell's bounds, where secrets dwell,
Reveal the witch, by this spell.
Through mist and time, let truth unfurl,
Guide our steps to her hidden world.

A pale cloud formed in the middle of our circle, one that seemed to begin resolving itself into the shape of a house. Just as quickly, though, it broke up and faded away, like a wall of mist getting blown apart by a sudden gust of wind.

"She has her house heavily warded," Valerie said. Her gray brows pulled together, but her voice sounded serene enough. "As I halfway expected. We will all need to place every ounce of our strength, of our magic, into making the spell as strong as it can possibly be."

Everyone in our little group nodded, and Elise's and my mother's grasps tightened on mine. Once again, we spoke the words of the spell in unison.

In Lowell's bounds, where secrets dwell,
Reveal the witch, by this spell.
Through mist and time, let truth unfurl,
Guide our steps to her hidden world.

And again the cloud formed between us, only this time it held steady, becoming more and more solid, at last showing us a large Victorian house that looked as if it had come out of Central Casting...if there was a Central Casting for houses. With its turret to one side and diamond-paned windows and its dark gray and deep red on black paint scheme, the place practically screamed that a witch lived there.

"Subtle," Stella murmured, and despite the tense situation, I couldn't quite hold back a chuckle.

"A distinctive house," Valerie said. "It shouldn't be too hard to track it down."

"Let me look it up online," Sage offered, and then reached inside the bag she still had slung over one shoulder so she could pull out her phone. A tense moment as she typed in the query and we looked on, and then she sent us all a relieved grin. "It's definitely in Lowell," she said. "It's sort of a tourist attraction, even though the gates are always shut and no one can get any closer than the road. But here's the address—1320 Hemlock Lane."

A fitting address for the home of a dark witch. Or at least, I assumed Larissa had come out ahead in that particular skirmish and had claimed the house as her own. She'd already shown she was willing to play very, very dirty.

"So, we know where she lives," I said. "Now what? Do we make some kind of frontal assault?"

"Oh, I'm sure Larissa is expecting something like that," Elise replied. "No, we have to be smart about this. I think the best thing to do is enlist the help of someone who has no reason to be on Larissa Richter's side."

"And who's that?" I asked, although a suspicion had already begun to flicker inside my mind.

Elise's mouth lifted, although I wasn't sure I could call the expression a smile. It had a little too much of a shark's humorless grin in it.

"Melissa Richter, Larissa's estranged sister, of course."

Chapter 14

Sisters Grim

"Do you know her?" I asked, and Elise shook her head.

"No," she replied calmly. "But I have to believe she'd be all too willing to help us out if it meant getting one up on her sister. We just have to find out where she is."

"On it," Sage said, and her thumbs flew over the screen of her phone as she entered the question in Google. A tense moment passed while we all waited, and then she gave us a relieved smile as she added, "It looks like she's in Lowell, too. The lawsuit over the house is still going on, which I suppose is why she didn't want to move too far away. It says here she's being represented by Dunbar, Hathaway, and Whitlock."

Of course. The same law firm where Adelaide Hanford worked. For all I knew, Adelaide was representing Melissa...and quite possibly had introduced her to her single brother, Milton. Maybe it wasn't the most charitable thought in the world, but I could see why Adelaide had thought it might be a good idea to have her brother date a woman who stood to inherit a sizable fortune.

All right, I was probably getting way ahead of myself, but I still thought the theory had some merit to it.

One thing I couldn't quite figure out was why Larissa had murdered Milton when it seemed as though her sister had already broken up with him. Well, that was something we could try to figure out later after we'd rescued Noah and Lexi and gotten Larissa taken care of, one way or another.

"Do you have an address for her?" I asked, and Sage's expression sank a little.

"No," she said. "I just know she's in Lowell because of the write-up I found about the lawsuit."

A hiccup, but not an insurmountable one. Luckily, though, we wouldn't have to reach out to the prickly Adelaide to get Melissa Richter's contact information.

No, magic could do that for us just fine.

Whispers of fate and threads that bind,
Reveal where Melissa Richter's signed.
In Lowell's embrace, where secrets rest,

Show her haven, her home, her nest.

"Okay, got it," I said after her address flickered briefly in the air, then disappeared. "Now what? Even if Melissa isn't exactly keen to help her sister, do you think it might be a little intimidating if all of us descended on her?"

"Oh, probably," my mother said, looking much more cheerful now that we had some kind of plan of attack in mind. "We all need to be nearby, because it will probably take all of us to defeat this dark witch, but I think it's better if you talk to her alone. We'll wait outside."

I had to believe that a group of seven women huddled near the apartment where Melissa Richter had taken up temporary residence would also be conspicuous, but it was still better than all of us trying to jam in there at once.

If she was even home at all. She could be at the grocery store, or her job—although I found that possibility slightly less likely, just because most witches preferred to be self-employed if at all possible, since that kind of setup made life a lot easier to navigate—or maybe even taking a walk. But we had to try. Worst case scenario, we'd wait until she got back.

And hope like hell that Larissa wasn't doing anything awful to Noah or Lexi. My brain kept manufacturing worse and worse scenarios, even though I told myself they were both valuable to her. After all, a dead vet couldn't perform the necessary surgery to remove the grimoire, and I knew Noah was smart enough to stall for time if he had to.

Except...he would have no reason to believe the cavalry was coming at all. He didn't know I was a witch, didn't know I was part of a coven determined to get him out of there no matter what. In that case, he might have cooperated and performed the surgery right away, thinking there wasn't anything else he could do.

That scenario didn't feel right to me, however. True, he didn't suspect me of being a witch...but he might have guessed that Larissa was the person who'd killed Milton Keyes. If he'd made that mental leap, then he would probably have done whatever he could to avoid removing the grimoire from Lexi's leg, since he'd have to believe the witch would most likely dispose of the two of them once she had what she wanted.

"Brooms or cars?" I asked. Broomsticks were a lot faster, but we generally tried to avoid flying together in large groups like this because even with a lot of "don't look at me" spells working together, you ran a much higher risk of being seen, especially in broad daylight like it was right now, with noon still almost an hour away.

"Cars," Elise replied promptly. "I know it's going to take about an hour to get to Lowell, but assuming everything goes well, we'll have both Noah and your dog to bring back with us. I know Stella could carry Noah, but the rest of us aren't as good at carrying extra weight on our brooms, and I think it's just safer to get there the nonmagical way."

Stella flushed a little at this indirect praise, but it was only the truth. She was definitely the fastest and best broom rider among us.

And, like the rest of us, she understood it was a lot harder to hide a broomstick against a clear blue sky.

That was why Milo, my mother, and Elise got in my Land Rover, while Grace drove Sage and Izzy and Valerie and Stella in her Ford Explorer. That left plenty of room in my car for Noah and Lexi, assuming we were successful at prying the two of them out of Larissa Richter's clutches.

Once we were out of Salem and on the interstate, I increased my speed, not to a point where I thought I'd attract the attention of any law enforcement in the vicinity, but just enough that I felt as if I was covering more ground than I would have otherwise. Milo and Elise sat in the back, while my mother occupied the front seat, although no one seemed too inclined toward conversation.

"Turn off on Beacon Street," my mother instructed me once we were inside Lowell's town limits, and I got over to the right and exited the highway. "Then a right onto Willard."

Once again, I followed her instructions, bringing us onto a small, quiet street with what looked like mostly townhouse and apartment complexes, backing up to a big structure I thought might be a grocery store. Because there were so many multi-unit buildings, parking lots dotted the area, making it easy for me to pull into one of the open spaces. A moment later, Grace's metallic blue Explorer slid into the spot next to mine.

I turned off the engine. "Okay, now that we've seen the place, what's the plan?"

Elise leaned forward from her spot in the back seat. "You go find Melissa Richter's townhouse. The rest of us will wait over there."

She pointed toward a cluster of large oak trees, their leaves just starting to shade into umber and brown. From what I could tell, the trees should provide enough shelter that it wouldn't be easy to see the group of women hiding behind them, while at the same time being close enough that they could come to my aid if necessary.

I had to hope that wouldn't happen, but just in case Melissa Richter's heart was as black as her sister's, it seemed better to have backup nearby.

"All right," I said, and glanced past Elise so my gaze could meet Milo's. Worry still wrinkled his brow, but there was also something alert about his stance, as if he was ready to leap into action at a moment's notice. "Time to go."

Even though they were doing their best to look inconspicuous, it wasn't that difficult to see the group of women...along with Milo, who'd reluctantly stayed with them rather than tag along at my side...huddled on the far side of the clump of trees. With any luck, anyone who saw them would think they'd met there before heading out for a late lunch, since it was now a little past one.

For myself, all I could do was walk along the path that wound through the townhouse complex and hope I looked as if I had every right to be there. I doubted anyone would suspect me of being a witch, not in the jeans and flats and black blouse I'd worn that day.

The unit Melissa Richter was renting sat smack in the middle of a row of other townhouses that looked identical, all of them painted pale yellow with white trim, each of them with a small enclosed patio area off a set of sliding glass doors and an even smaller balcony adorning the second floor.

No time to waste on being nervous. I reached out and pressed the doorbell button, then waited.

A moment later, a woman opened the door,

someone who looked so much like the witch who'd appeared in Noah's clinic and spirited him away that I barely stopped myself from letting out a gasp and taking a step backward. Somehow, I managed to stay where I was and say, "Melissa Richter?"

"Yes," she replied, now frowning a little, as if she was trying to place where she might have seen me before. Now that I faced her more or less squarely, I could see that, while her features were somewhat similar to her sister's, with the same chiseled nose and big brown eyes, her expression was utterly different, her mouth lacking the pinched quality I'd noticed in Larissa's face. "Can I help you?"

"It's about your sister," I said, and at once her expression seemed to shut down.

"My sister and I are currently involved in litigation," she said crisply. "I don't have anything to say about her."

"Even if I told you she has the grimoire?"

At once, Melissa Richter's eyes flared open in shock. "How do you know about that?"

"I know a lot of things," I said. "Because I'm a witch, just like you. Can I please come inside?"

She hesitated for a second, then said, "All right," and stepped out of the way.

The townhouse was small, with a cramped living room and an equally inadequate kitchen. The carpet was beige, and so was the furniture. I got the feeling she'd rented this place furnished because she'd been turned out of the family house with basically nothing, and had probably chosen the first halfway suitable place she could find.

No offer for me to sit, only, "You really think Larissa found the grimoire?"

"I know she did," I replied. "I'm the one who took Lexi in. My name's Charity Hughes."

Once again, Melissa's eyes widened, only this time, I thought it was with recognition. "I hoped Lexi would make it to you...but I didn't dare get too close in case Larissa was watching what I was doing. The only thing I could do was place a very small enchantment on the dog to make it more likely that she'd end up in your care."

Well, that explained why Lexi had come to me rather than the local animal shelter. And considering what Larissa Richter was capable of, I had to be glad of Melissa's caution in approaching me. "Yes, I got to take Lexi in," I said. "The man I'm seeing is a vet, and it was while he was examining her that he found the grimoire."

"It was the only thing I could think of to do," Melissa said, her voice ragged, not much more than a whisper. "I had no idea that Larissa would think to find the grimoire hidden in the dog, especially since it had been almost two months since Milton and I split up."

Those last words cracked a little as she spoke,

and I saw tears shining in her brown eyes. Clearly, she knew exactly what had happened to the man she'd dated.

Before I could attempt to make a consoling comment, though, she went on, "I didn't want to end things. Larissa told me it was stupid to get involved with a man at this stage of my life when it wasn't as if I could have a child to carry on the family line. No, she said I needed to be paying attention to much more important things. And since Mother was sick...."

The words trailed off, but I thought I could read between the lines.

"Your mother was sick, and then she passed away and left you and your sister the house," I said, doing my best to keep my tone gentle, even though my brain was prodding me to move things along so we could go rescue Noah and Lexi.

But, to my surprise, Melissa shook her head. "No, she left the house to me. She knew what kind of magic Larissa had been playing with and didn't approve at all. The grimoire had been passed down from generation to generation, but no one in my family had used it for centuries, fearing the spells it contained. Larissa, though...she wanted it. She wanted it badly. One of the last things my mother asked of me was to hide it from my sister. So I did."

"And that was why Larissa went to Milton's antique shop and asked if he had it?"

"She did that?" Again, Melissa continued before I had a chance to respond. "But yes, I suppose she might have thought I'd hidden it among the antiques, even though Milton and I were no longer seeing each other. Now I can see why she was so angry when she came home that day. Our mother had passed away about a week earlier, but even though Larissa searched the entire house, she couldn't find the grimoire. She confronted me, too, and I finally got the courage to tell her that I'd allowed her to stay in the house because she'd suffered a loss as well, but that Mother had left it to me, not her, and it was time to go."

"I assume she didn't take that very well," I said dryly.

Melissa's mouth twitched. "No. And then she told me the house was hers and showed me the will, which had been magically altered to make it look as if everything had been left to her. I tried to take it away from her and see if I could change it back, but she just laughed and said I had better leave if I didn't want something much worse to happen to me." Looking a little shamefaced, she added, "Her magic was always much stronger than mine, even without the grimoire. But if she has it now...."

"She has Lexi," I said, my tone urgent. "And she has Noah, my boyfriend." I paused there before asking, "How was she able to find them, anyway?"

"I don't know for sure," Melissa replied. "Some kind of tracking spell, most likely. After I realized what she'd done to Milton"—a pause there while she pulled in a hitch of a breath, eyes glittering with tears I knew she wouldn't allow to fall—"I went to the house and took Lexi and brought her to Salem, hoping that would keep her out of harm's way. And it did…for a while. But then Larissa must have guessed the dog was involved somehow, and would have bent all her magic toward finding her."

That explanation made some sense. However, because I didn't see the need to continue speculating on what Larissa might or might not have done with her magic, not with Noah and Lexi in her clutches, I said, "I'm sure Larissa took my boyfriend so she could force him to perform surgery on the dog to extract the grimoire. We need to get to them now—he might have already done it, because she took them more than an hour ago."

Melissa's face was pale. "I don't think I can help you," she said, her voice quiet, defeated. "If that much time has passed, then she has the grimoire and doesn't need your boyfriend or the dog anymore."

"But you miniaturized the grimoire, right?" I pressed. No way in the world was I going to give up this easily, not when I now stood only a mile or so from the spot where Noah and Lexi were being held captive. "How easy is it to reverse that spell?"

"Not easy at all," she replied, and she sounded a little stronger now, not quite so hopeless. "My mother taught it to me, but Larissa never learned it, nor the proper way to reverse the magic in order to return an item that had been shrunk to its normal size. She would have thought something like that was fiddly and useless."

But it wasn't useless...far from it. The enchantment had allowed Melissa to hide the grimoire in Lexi, and I had to hope it was the one thing currently preventing Larissa from expanding the book of dark magic and using its contents for her own ends.

"Then we still have time," I said. "I brought my coven with me, and I'm sure that all of us working together will be enough to defeat your sister and take the grimoire away from her."

And get you your house back, I thought grimly. No, that hadn't been the purpose of this mission, but if my fellow witches and I came out ahead in this confrontation, I had to hope there was some way we could also change the will back to its original form and prove that Larissa Richter had no business squatting in the house on Hemlock Lane.

No, her new digs should be a jail cell, but the only way we could make that work would be to have Elise perform her pineal-destroying "surgery" once again.

Once again, a flicker of hope came and went in Melissa's dark eyes. "How many in your coven?"

"Eight," I replied.

"And if I join with you, that will be nine."

A number we'd had in our witchy group until we had to remove Tonya, thanks to her numerous crimes. But if Melissa cast her lot in with us....

"Yes," I said, praying inwardly that she'd agree to join my coven to face down her awful sister. "It would be a huge help if you worked with us. That would have to be enough to beat your sister, wouldn't it?"

For a moment, Melissa didn't answer. Her gaze moved past me, taking in the shabby townhouse, the used furniture, as if comparing them to the home and the furnishings Larissa had stolen from her.

"All right," she said at last. "I'm in."

The two us headed over to meet the rest of my coven. As soon as Valerie spied Melissa and me approaching, she must have guessed the interview had gone well, because she stepped out from the shelter of the trees, and the rest of the group followed her. Once again, I had to be glad all this was taking place in the middle of the day and not when the people who occupied these apartments and townhouses were coming home from school, since otherwise we probably would have presented a fairly odd picture.

"This is Melissa," I said as she and I paused a little ways away from the Salem coven. "She's going to help us get into the house her sister stole from her."

At those words, Valerie's eyebrows lifted, and I noticed how my mother and the other members of the group shot startled glances at one another. However, no one spoke, telling me they understood this wasn't the time for a lot of unnecessary questions.

"She'll have the place warded," Melissa said, also seeming to realize that we couldn't waste even a minute on making introductions. "But all of us working together should be able to get past those without too much trouble. I think the best way to approach the house is from the rear—it backs up onto a small wood without any homes, and there's a door off the kitchen that opens onto the garden. There's less chance she'll be back there, since she uses the study for all her magic workings. I'm sure the study is where she must be keeping Lexi and Charity's boyfriend."

Obviously, Larissa wasn't a kitchen witch, but I could have already guessed that.

"Any wards on the interior of the house?" Elise inquired.

"There didn't used to be," Melissa replied. "But I haven't lived there for almost a month, so I have no idea what Larissa might have done during the time I was gone."

Not the best news, and it seemed everyone thought the same thing, since I noticed the way Stella and Izzy and Sage frowned, how Elise's mouth pursed.

"But even if she's cast some wards, I doubt they'd be stronger than the ones she would have put in place on the outside of the house," Melissa said. "She always hated how the house was on the historic register and how people would come by to take pictures of it. That's why she always made sure the exterior was warded—she didn't want anyone to get too close."

While I otherwise didn't think I had anything in common with Larissa Richter, I had to agree that I might have done the exact same thing if I'd been in her position. Witches by their very nature were private creatures; none of us wanted our magical doings to be discovered by the public. My house wasn't a tourist attraction—and I wouldn't have bought it if it had been—so luckily, I didn't have to worry about that kind of thing.

"Well," my mother said briskly, speaking for the first time, "we'll deal with any wards inside the house if and when we encounter them. I think the best thing to do now is get over there and get Lexi and Noah away before Larissa can cause any more harm."

Everyone agreed on that suggestion, so we all headed for my and Grace's cars, with Melissa taking shotgun in the Discovery so she could navigate while I drove and Grace could follow.

It turned out the Richters' ancestral home wasn't too far from the place she'd been renting, probably not even a mile as the crow flies. However, it was distant enough to take us out of the town center and to a lovely neighborhood of historic homes, each of them sitting on large lots, with the black Victorian where Melissa had once lived at the end of the street.

As she'd described, it backed up onto a lovely little wooded area. She instructed me to cut down a small lane that dead-ended at a trail head, although it didn't look as though anyone else was using it on this particular Friday afternoon.

"You can't see this parking area from the house," Melissa explained as my mother and Elise and Milo got out of the back seat. "That's why I thought it would be safer to leave the cars here. And it's only a couple of hundred yards to get to the back fence."

"Lead on," I told her, and the rest of us fell in behind her—with Milo sticking close to my side—as we threaded our way through the little grove of white pine and oak and hemlock.

Sure enough, we only had to walk for a few minutes before we reached the fence Melissa had mentioned. It was an elaborate wrought-iron affair, painted black to match the house, with frightening arrowhead-shaped points sitting on top of each post. Needless to say, it didn't look very climbable.

Well, that was where being a witch came in handy. We all could use magic to allow ourselves to hop over the barrier, with no broomsticks required.

Assuming we got past the wards, of course.

Melissa spread her arms wide, eyes closed, as though she was listening to the wind...or maybe just trying to sense any magic in the vicinity.

"Yes, it's warded," she said in a dreamy voice. "Can you sense it?"

Elise stepped forward and also reached out, fingers spread wide, obviously doing her best to pick up any magical vibes nearby. "Oh, yes," she said, although her tone was brisk and matter-of-fact, a direct contrast to Melissa's. "I can feel it. It's strong," she added over her shoulder, addressing those words to the rest of us. "But I think we can manage it. Let's join hands."

At once we formed a circle, with Melissa joining in so we could reach the magically charged number of nine. I could practically feel the energy thrumming amongst us, making me wonder if it was her presence that had given our group a little extra charge.

Good. We were going to need it.

Barrier of shadows, ward of night,
Your strength dissolves in my sight.
By my word, let this fence be clear,
Open the path, let no more interfere.

We all waited for Melissa to speak after the spell had been cast, since it was clear she was much better equipped to detect her sister's magic and know whether we'd disabled it. Her lips pursed, and then she shook her head.

"Let's try again," she said. "I think we weakened it a little, but it's still there."

I wouldn't allow myself to be disappointed. These things could take time, even though once again, I couldn't ignore the way it seemed as if the minutes and seconds were slipping past, faster and faster.

Anything could be happening inside that house.

My mother's fingers tightened on mine, as if she could sense my inner impatience and was silently admonishing me to take a breath and focus.

I didn't nod, but I thought she understood that her message had gotten through. On my other side, Stella stood tall and sure, chin up, golden blonde hair bright in the September sunshine. Kai must be watching the baby, which made me wonder if they'd had to close Tea & Sympathy while she was out on this rescue mission.

Focus, I told myself.

Melissa began to speak again, this time using an old, old spell of unbinding, attempting to unravel the ward rather than break through it. The rest of us picked up the words, joining our voices to hers even as our magic blended and mingled once more.

Veil of magic, tightly wound,
Hear my call, to unbind this round.
From this fence, release your hold,
Let your secrets now unfold.

Once we were done, Melissa went still. While she didn't exactly smile, satisfaction was clear on her face.

"That did it," she said. "Now, up and over —quick."

No time to stop and think. I uttered a charm under my breath that would allow me to bounce over the fence as though I'd launched myself from a trampoline, and everyone else did the same as well. Under other circumstances, I might have chuckled to see plump Grace Bowersby doing her "man in the moon" leap, or dignified Elise Figg with her Indian-print skirt fluttering in the air.

Now, though, I just wanted to keep moving.

However, I wasn't in such a hurry that I hadn't

stopped to cast one of my "don't look at me spells," and I knew everyone else in the group had done the same. Whether it would actually protect us from Larissa Richter's magical eyes, I didn't know, but at least it kept anyone who might have decided to wander along the trail from seeing a bunch of grown women floating through the air.

Soon enough, we were across the manicured yard—set up like a formal English garden, with gravel walks and carefully trimmed rosebushes—and approaching the back door. Melissa took the lead as she crept up the steps and put her hand on the back door's latch.

"It's locked," she said in an undertone. "But that shouldn't be a problem."

Sure enough, the door opened as she pressed down on the handle.

"The study is on the ground floor," she went on, still in that same near-murmur. "Through the kitchen, and then the second door on the left. Is everyone ready?"

She glanced around our little group, and everyone nodded in reply.

"Then let's go."

None of us made a sound as we moved out of the kitchen and down the hallway beyond. Once again, I knew our utter quiet was due more to the various stealth charms we'd cast than because any of us was particularly good at sneaking around in other people's houses, but it still helped, allowing us to creep up to the door Melissa had indicated, which stood open. I couldn't hear any sound coming from within, which didn't seem like a very good sign to me.

Were we too late?

But then a shadow fell across the doorway, and Larissa Richter stepped onto the threshold, a smile that was mostly a sneer tugging at her lips. Looking at her now, I realized that, while she and Melissa had the same coloring and slightly similar features, they definitely weren't mirror images of each other. Fraternal twins, then, not identical.

"Hello," Larissa said, still wearing that unpleasant smirk. "I thought you'd show up eventually."

Chapter 15

Stay a Spell

Even though I was surrounded by my fellow coven members, I couldn't quite stop the shiver that tickled its way down my spine. Larissa looked very sure of herself, even though she was outnumbered nine to one.

"You need to let them go," Melissa said. Her chin had lifted in defiance, and if she was at all afraid, she definitely didn't show it. "There's no excuse for anything you've done."

Larissa's dark eyes widened with mock innocence. "What *have* I done, exactly? Come in—you'll see they're utterly unharmed."

I didn't believe that comment for a second... and neither did anyone else in the coven, judging by the skeptical expressions they wore. However, since Larissa stepped out of the way, we all went inside the study.

It was a large room with bookcases on every wall except one that I guessed faced west, since the sun would have been glaring right into the space if a large elm tree hadn't been blocking most of the light. Because of that, it took my eyes a second or two to become accustomed to the gloom.

In the center of the room was a round table, and on that table lay Lexi. She didn't move, and for one horrifying second, I thought she might be dead.

But then I saw her little furry sides rise and fall slowly, and realized she must be caught in some kind of paralysis spell, maybe the same one Larissa had used on me to steal Noah and the dog away. To my additional relief, it didn't look as though she'd been harmed or touched at all, which meant Noah must have defied Larissa somehow and refused to operate on the dog to remove the grimoire.

And there he was, thank all the powers in the universe, sitting in a chair a few feet away from the table where Lexi lay on her side. His eyes were wide with fear and a kind of impotent fury, and even as my heart burned with anguish over what he'd gone through, I guessed Larissa had also paralyzed him to prevent him from trying to attack her in some way. No, the man I loved wasn't prone to violence, but he probably had realized the only way to possibly save himself and Lexi was to strike out at the evil woman who'd kidnapped them.

But at least he appeared unharmed, which was something. Now we just had to get him and the dog...and the rest of us...out of there. I did my best to send him an encouraging look, to let him know the cavalry had arrived, even though his current paralysis really wouldn't let him respond to me in any tangible way.

"You've done enough," Melissa said. She'd told us her sister was the stronger witch by far, and yet I thought having the rest of us with her had given her the courage to confront her quite literally evil twin. "You killed Milton. And I have no doubt you would have killed these two once you'd gotten what you wanted."

"He wasn't good enough for you," Larissa responded. "And far too old. Really, I did you a favor."

Her expression and tone were utterly unconcerned, as if she'd done nothing more than warn the man off rather than brutally murder him and rip his heart out of his chest.

Elise stepped forward. She, too, looked unruffled, but then, she probably had a better idea of what we were up against here, since she also played with dark magic from time to time, if not to the extent that Larissa did.

"What did you do with his heart?" she asked, her tone indicating nothing but mild curiosity. "I have my ideas, but I'm curious, especially since it seems as if you'd already successfully broken up the relationship."

Larissa lifted an eyebrow. "That, I fear, is privileged information." She sent a similarly contemptuous glance toward the rest of our little group, telling me she'd allowed us in here because she truly thought she'd be able to best our coven despite the overwhelming numbers arrayed against her. "It was very sweet of you to come to your friend's rescue, but he has something I need, and I'm tired of his stubbornness...and your interference."

A hand went up, and at once, a terrible, knifing pain went through me, so awful that for a second, I thought I was having a heart attack. Next to me, Sage doubled over, her face white with fear.

Right then, I guessed exactly what Larissa had done with Milton's heart—she'd used it for a component in a dark spell that would make its victims feel as if they were dying of what people sometimes referred to as a widow-maker.

But although Elise's face was tight with pain, she still managed a lopsided smile. "Interesting," she said, "but we know this is only an illusion."

My mother's hand found mine, and my fingers wrapped around Sage's. Within a second or two, our coven—along with Melissa—had joined forces.

Time for a little payback.

Nothing fancy, just a sheer wall of force that

surged forth from us and hit Larissa square in the chest. She staggered backward a few steps, face contorting in pain and shock.

I got the feeling she wasn't expecting a motley group of witches like us to summon that kind of energy…or that her sister would join us in conjuring it.

But the problem with attacking someone who dealt in dark magic was that they knew how to counter-punch.

Her hand went out, and in the next second, a cloud of spiders fell from the ceiling, descending on us. I could feel tiny legs wriggling in my hair, down the back of my shirt.

No thought then, just a raw, atavistic reaction. Before that moment, I wouldn't have called myself an arachnophobe—I was the kind of person who put spiders outside rather than squishing them—but all I could think of was to drop to the floor and roll around, fingers pulling at my hair, doing my best to smash the ones that had somehow found their way down my blouse.

Even the normally cool and collected Elise looked frantic, swatting at one that crawled down her cheek, twisting and contorting as she tried to get away from the arachnoid attackers, while next to me, Sage had fallen to the floor and whimpered as she shook her head violently this way and that, trying to dislodge the spiders wriggling through her hair.

Larissa smirked again, clearly thinking she'd found the one way to defeat us.

Was it an illusion? Did it matter?

I really didn't know what might have happened next, except then Milo barked and lunged at Larissa, slamming into her legs so she was knocked off her feet.

At once, the spiders disappeared, telling me that yes, they had been an illusion. And before Larissa could react, her sister had stepped forward.

"Give her a taste of her own medicine!" she cried. "She won't be able to do anything if she's paralyzed, too!"

Our group scrambled to their feet and joined hands. Elise was the one who spoke the words of the spell, but all of us sent our energy to her, ensuring the enchantment would be stronger than anything she could have cast on her own.

With power drawn from depths untold,
We bind thee now in folds of cold.
Let muscles lock and limbs grow still,
By our command, by our will.

At once, Larissa went utterly motionless, lying so flat on the ground, you would have thought she was playing that old "light as a feather, stiff as a board" game from back in grade school.

Although I kind of got the impression that Larissa hadn't been much for schoolgirl games… except maybe "Bloody Mary."

"Stand her up," Melissa said, a new note of command in her voice, and Sage and Stella, younger and nimbler than the other coven members, went to grasp Larissa by the shoulders and heave her upright, where they placed her up against the nearest set of bookshelves.

Her dark eyes spat fire, but it looked as if the spell was holding, so she couldn't do much more than stand there, immobile, and glare at us.

My mother put her hands on her hips. "What now?"

She sounded tired, and I couldn't blame her. After that spider attack, adrenaline still twinged and twanged along all my nerve endings, and my hands and legs couldn't stop shaking.

Elise looked drained as well…and wary. I had to guess she was also thinking the only thing we could do now was zap Larissa's pineal gland the way we had Tonya Willis's so Larissa wouldn't be able to work her dark magic ever again.

However, it seemed Melissa had other plans. She went over to the table where Lexi had lain, quiet and still, this entire time, and laid a hand on the dog's head, gently touching her ears. Then she ran that same hand down the length of the dog's body until it at last came to rest on the same haunch where she'd hidden the grimoire.

Not even a tremble, but a second later, the miniaturized grimoire appeared on the witch's palm.

"This should help with most of it," she said, her tone quiet but with a note of steel in it nonetheless.

From whispers small to presence grand,
Expand beneath my open hand.
What once was miniaturized, arise,
Grow forth and reach your normal size.

The tiny book in her hand—even smaller than the kind of books I'd seen in fancy dollhouses—was much too large to hold in one's palm once it had been expanded to its actual size. Instead, Melissa grasped it with both hands and took it over to the desk, all while Larissa continued to glare at her twin sister with the kind of fire in her eyes that would have spelled certain death...if she hadn't been immobilized and unable to use any of her magic.

I'd never seen a grimoire before, had only read about them, but even if I hadn't known what the book of spells was, I would have still been able to sense the enormous power that seemed to radiate from its worn black binding, from the heavily illustrated pages within. Melissa leafed through it, clearly looking for a certain spell.

Then she paused and glanced up at the rest of us, expression bleak. "I don't know if I can do this."

Because of course she thought the only way to truly neutralize her sister's awful magic was to end her life…no matter what performing such a terrible, black act of magic might cost her.

Elise stepped forward and laid a hand on Melissa's arm. "You don't have to. There's another way."

A terrible hope bloomed in the other woman's face, and I knew then that although she'd thought she had no choice but to permanently remove her sister from the equation, we might be able to help her here.

After all, we'd faced a similar situation when dealing with Tonya Willis not so long ago.

"Our magic resides in the pineal gland," Elise said, her voice calm, almost thoughtful. "If we burn out Larissa's, she'll be an ordinary mortal. She won't remember anything about the powers she once possessed, and all the spells she cast will die along with her magic."

Melissa blinked, then glanced over at me, the look on her face telling me how much she wanted to believe what Elise was saying…and also that she wasn't quite sure she could.

"It's true," I said gently. I glanced over at Noah, who remained unnaturally still, and who would stay that way until the spell was lifted...one way or another. He now looked stunned as well as angry, his clear blue eyes full of questions.

There was a conversation I wasn't looking forward to having, even though I knew I couldn't avoid it. Not after everything Noah had just gone through. I owed him the truth about everything, even though I had no idea how I could make any of this better.

But first, we needed to deal with Larissa Richter.

"I can take care of it," Elise said. "I've done this before."

Melissa gave her a small, humorless smile. "No, I want to help. I want to be a part of taking her magic away. After what she did to Milton...."

The words trailed off, since she obviously thought it wasn't necessary to finish the sentence.

"That's fair," Elise replied. "You can lend your powers to mine as I recite the words of the spell."

A grim nod. "Good. That way, I can look Larissa in the face while it's happening."

Her tone was almost matter-of-fact, but I saw the way her eyes glittered with barely contained rage. She wanted her sister to know exactly what they were doing to her...right up until the moment when all memory of magic was taken away from her forever.

Elise pressed her lips together, but I could tell she wasn't going to comment. Instead, she said in carefully neutral tones, "Then let's get this done."

She reached one hand out to Melissa, who grasped it tightly. A moment of silence, while Larissa glared at the two women with such malice that I could only pray the petrification spell would hold her until this done, and then Elise's lips parted again.

By moon's decree and starlight's grace,
I strip your power from this place.
Witch's magic, now undone,
In darkness, you'll be left with none.

The glare Larissa had been directing at her sister and Elise turned oddly glassy, as if the will that had been powering it had been cut off at the source. Her face was as blank and empty as a doll's, and I knew in that moment that her magic was gone, destroyed at its source, just as Tonya Willis's had been.

At once, I looked over at Noah, but he still remained motionless, jaw tight, limbs unmoving. Why hadn't the spell been broken? Larissa's magic was gone, wasn't it?

Before I could say anything, however, my mother spoke up.

"Larissa is going to be...not herself...for some time," she said. "The question is, what do you want to do next?"

"Have her arrested for Milton's murder," Melissa replied at once. "But will she even remember what she did?"

"Hard to say," Elise put in. "A lot of things will be foggy for her, since she used her magic so often. But she should remain highly suggestible for a while. It won't be too hard to let her know the best thing she can do is confess to killing Milton Keyes."

A nod, and Melissa said, "That sounds like a good plan."

Valerie asked then, her tone gentle, "Is there anything else you need us to help you with?"

The other woman didn't answer at first, only gazed around our circle as if committing our faces to memory. "You've already helped me," she said. "More than you can ever know. I would never have been able to do this without your assistance."

Maybe not. Maybe it had taken our combined strength to give Melissa Richter the extra push she needed to confront her terrible sister...and make sure Larissa received the justice she deserved.

"I won't forget," Melissa went on, then, to my surprise, laid her hand against her stomach. "And neither will she."

I stared at her wide-eyed, while all around me, my fellow coven members did the same.

"You're going to have a child?" my mother said, asking the same question that clearly had leaped into all our minds.

Melissa nodded. "Yes. She's Milton's. I thought —well, I suspected for a while, but I knew these kinds of things aren't as easy after you hit forty. But I went to see a doctor a week ago, and she confirmed the pregnancy. That was part of the reason why I tried to stay away from Larissa, and why I hired Adelaide's firm to get my part of the inheritance returned. I knew Larissa would be furious with me for having Milton's child, but I also knew this house was my daughter's birthright. I had to fight to get it back."

My head was spinning. Not because I didn't believe anything of what Melissa was saying, but that she would be brave enough to confront her sister when she knew exactly how much was at stake.

How it wasn't just her life she was defending.

An explosive little sneeze made us all turn. Lexi stood on the table where she'd been lying just a moment earlier, looking perplexed.

And then she barked. A small bark, more questioning than anything else, but....

"Lexi?" I said. "Are you all right, little girl?"

She shook, one of those doggy shakes that

seemed to start at the tip of her nose and go all the way down to her tail, and barked again.

"She can't talk!" Milo exclaimed. After knocking Larissa to the floor, he'd hurried back to my side, just in case I needed any additional defending. "What's the matter with her?"

Everyone was looking at him, puzzled, because of course they couldn't understand him.

Only I could...and I thought I knew the answer to his question, even though I really hated to have to deliver such bad news.

"Larissa was the one who cast the spell on Lexi to make her talk," I explained. "So when her magic was taken away, the spell disappeared as well."

Milo's ears drooped. "But we were friends."

"I know, sweetie," I said. "The problem is, Lexi's not a familiar. She's just an ordinary dog."

Melissa stepped out from behind the desk, expression curiously understanding. "He wants to know why Lexi can't talk anymore, right?"

I nodded. "They got to be good friends. So he's just sad right now that he won't be able to talk to her like they used to. I'm sure we'll all get used to it eventually."

To my surprise, Melissa actually smiled. "I think we can do better than that. You're going to keep Lexi, aren't you?"

"That was the plan," I replied, even as I once again looked over at Noah, who still remained motionless, Larissa's spell somehow keeping him immobile. Jaw tight with frustration—could we break the enchantment if it didn't fade on its own? —I added, "But she was Milton's dog. I can understand if you want to keep her for yourself."

"No," Melissa said firmly. "I mean, I got along well with Lexi, but I've never owned a dog...and my hands are going to be pretty full in the coming months." Once again, her hand stole to her still-flat stomach, as if to reassure herself of the child she carried. "It's better that Lexi goes to live with you. And I don't want to deprive Milo of his friend."

Another smile, and she returned to the grimoire, then flipped a few pages. When she spoke, it was to utter the kind of spell I knew all of us wanted to hear.

Voice of silence, now set free,
Grant this dog the gift to speak to me.
From this moment, let her voice be clear,
Words unbound, for all witches to hear.

At once, the little dog's long, feathery tail began to wag, and her big brown eyes lit up. "I can talk!"

"Yes, you can," I said as I went over to her so I could carefully set her down on the floor. Immediately, Milo hurried to Lexi and pressed his nose against hers, both their tails wagging at lightspeed. I looked up from the dogs and back at Melissa as I added, "Thank you so much."

"I'm glad I could help." Her smile faded then as she seemed to catch sight of her sister, still propped against the bookcase, her expression blank and wondering. "I need to call the police, and better to do it soon while Larissa still isn't herself."

True enough. Tonya had been pretty out of it for a few days after Elise zonked her pineal gland, but Larissa had been an even more powerful witch. It was possible she'd bounce back more quickly, and doubly important that the authorities got her confession on file before she had a change of heart.

At last, Noah got up from his chair at last, looking a little wobbly. I didn't know for sure why it had taken a bit longer for his paralysis spell to wear off, except he was much bigger than Lexi, and Larissa had probably made the enchantment extra strong just to be safe, binding it to him over and over again so there was no chance of his ever escaping. He might not have been a witch, but he was still strong and fit and could have given her a whole lot of trouble if she hadn't made sure her magic held him fast.

Milo and Lexi hurried over to him, tails wagging faster than ever, and although he sent me a look that was scalpel sharp, it seemed he wasn't willing to get into it in front of everybody, especially with two dogs begging for his attention.

Instead, he bent and petted both of them, murmuring that they were good dogs. Judging by the worried glances the members of my coven shot me then, I knew they weren't sure how to handle the situation. Yes, every witch who decided to settle down with a partner revealed the truth to them at some point, but in this particular case, I was being pretty much forced into it.

Well, we'd deal with that later. For now, we needed to get out of there so Melissa could alert the authorities and have them take her sister away. What would happen next, with her mother's will in such a tangle thanks to Larissa's meddling, I wasn't sure. Some kind of lengthy probate, I guessed. What exactly happened when someone involved in a civil case was arrested for murder?

I had absolutely no idea. But Melissa had Adelaide Hanford working for her, and I was pretty sure she would make mincemeat of any bureaucrats who tried to get between her client and her inheritance...especially when that client was expecting a child.

We all hurried out of the study and to the back fence, where one by one, my coven members launched themselves up and over the barrier as if it didn't exist.

Noah's eyes met mine, and I swallowed.

"I can get you over," I said, doing my best to sound completely neutral. "But it'll be easier if you can carry one of the dogs. You can take Lexi."

"Sure," he said, his tone stiffer than I'd ever heard it. "I can do that."

He bent and picked up the little dog, who wore a confused expression, as though she couldn't quite understand why he was sounding so cold.

But I could.

I'd have to deal with that later, though. For now, we just needed to get away and back to Salem.

A quick charm to lift Noah up and over the fence, and then I looked down at Milo.

"He's angry with you, isn't he?"

"Yes," I said, marveling a little at how calm I sounded. "But I'm sure we can work things out. Right now, though, I need to pick you up."

The dog appeared resigned, which didn't surprise me too much. Although he loved being petted and cuddled, he wasn't much for being carried. I got the impression he thought it was beneath his dignity.

But there wasn't much else we could do right now. I leaned over and gathered him in my arms, and a moment later, we were on the other side of the fence with everyone else.

"Back to the cars," my mother said briskly, obviously doing her best to ignore the simmering tension between Noah and me.

And since he'd clearly decided it wouldn't be

the best idea to pick a fight with me in front of everyone...not to mention running the risk of getting stranded here in Lowell if he pissed me off enough...he didn't say anything, only followed my mother and me, Lexi still in his arms and a grim expression on his face.

No one said anything. I wasn't sure what would have been worse—some kind of inane chatter to break the tension, or this painful silence.

However, we eventually made it to the parking area for the trailhead. Izzy, Sage, Stella, and Valerie all followed Grace over to her SUV, leaving me to lead the remainder of our group to my Land Rover.

"Noah, you can ride up front," I said. "Mom, Elise—take Milo with you to the back."

No one argued with those arrangements, probably because Noah was a good bit taller than any of the rest of us, and it just made sense for him to sit where there was more legroom. Milo didn't look too happy—he loved riding shotgun—but he must have realized I couldn't indulge him right now.

The ride back to Salem was just as silent and tense as the walk to the cars had been. I kept my eyes fixed on the road, not daring to look over at Noah, who continued to hold Lexi the entire time.

I dropped off my mother and Elise first—easy enough, since they lived on the same street—and then said, still looking forward, "Do you want me to take you home, or do you want to go to my house?"

"My place, please," he replied, so stiff and formal, his voice barely sounded like his.

The sort of response I'd been expecting, but still, I couldn't help heaving an inner sigh.

This wasn't going well at all.

I pulled up into his driveway and turned off the engine. Before I could say anything, Noah spoke.

"I think we need to talk."

Chapter 16

Aftermath

Noah finally set Lexi down after he stepped out of my SUV, and Milo jumped out when I opened the rear door for him. The dog seemed to realize this wasn't the time to be boisterous, because he waited sedately while Noah headed up the front steps and unlocked the door.

It had only been a couple of days since I was last here, but something about the house felt unfamiliar to me, almost foreign.

Or maybe I was getting that impression because of the bleak expression the man I loved continued to wear.

However, he hadn't lost himself in his anger so much that he didn't pour a bowl of water for Milo and Lexi, and then crack the back door so they could go out into the yard. In fact, the significant glance he sent Milo seemed to be enough for the dogs to understand that they needed to head outside so the two of us could be alone.

Which they did, after Milo nudged Lexi with his nose, letting her know that their people needed some privacy.

"So, you're a witch," Noah said, his tone flat.

There wasn't much point in denying it, not after everything he'd seen at the Richter house.

"Yes," I replied.

"And so are your mother and Sage and all those other women."

It wasn't a question.

"Yes," I said again. "We're all part of the same coven."

He blinked at that word, then reached up to push back a lock of wavy brown hair that had fallen forward over his forehead. "Were you ever going to tell me?"

Oh, boy. I pulled in a breath and said, "Maybe we should sit down."

For a moment, it felt as if he was going to protest, was going to tell me he wanted to have it out right here in the kitchen, but then he seemed to relent.

"All right."

We headed into the living room, where he sat down on the sofa. I wasn't brave enough to take a seat next to him, so instead I settled myself on the nearby accent chair.

"I would have told you...eventually," I said.

His jaw tightened. "How eventually?"

This was not the way I'd intended to have this conversation. "After I was sure."

"Sure about what?"

"About us," I said slowly.

"So...you weren't sure? You thought our relationship was casual?"

He spoke calmly, but I could hear the clipped anger behind his words.

"That's not what I said," I returned, then made myself breathe in again. Maybe the cause was already lost, but I didn't want to give in to impatience or anger, not when I was the one who'd been concealing so much of myself from him. "I don't think it was casual at all. But still...we witches have had to hide the magical sides of ourselves from the world for centuries. We have to be very, very careful before we tell anyone on the outside who we are, what we can do. The risks are just too great otherwise."

A flicker in his blue eyes, one I couldn't quite interpret. "So...I'm on the outside?"

"It's just a way of saying people who aren't born to witch families. That's all."

He leaned forward, hands pressed against his

jean-clad knees. "So...this kind of thing is hereditary?"

Still not exactly a neutral topic, but better than discussing our relationship and whether we even still had one at all. "Yes," I replied. "It goes from mother to daughter. Witches always have girls."

Better to leave it there, even though the situation was much more complicated than that. I didn't think I had the mental energy to explain what happened when our hereditary magic encountered a Y chromosome.

Noah seemed to absorb that detail for a moment. He still wore that almost blank expression, as if he was doing his best not to reveal anything of what he was thinking.

"And Milo is your familiar?"

"Not exactly," I said. "His bond to his witch—Darla Fitzgerald—wasn't very strong, so when she was murdered, he didn't perish with her. Because I can talk to familiars, I took him in."

A tilt of the head, as if his gaze had strayed to the window where I could see Milo and Lexi happily nosing around one of the flowerbeds.

Not for the first time, I thought it might be nice to be a dog. If nothing else, that kind of existence seemed a lot less complicated.

"So...Lexi's a familiar, too?"

"No," I said. "She's just a regular dog with a

spell cast on her to allow her to talk. I think Larissa performed the original enchantment because she wanted to see if she could learn from Lexi where the grimoire had been hidden, but Melissa revived the speech spell when she saw how much we all liked having the dog be able to talk."

Now Noah reached up to rub his forehead, as if all this talk of spells and enchantments had made his head start to hurt. I couldn't really blame him —it was a lot to take in.

"And everyone can talk to familiars?"

"No," I said. "It's a special gift I have. That's why I foster so many animals—it's because their mistresses ask me to work with them if they're having some kind of issue. I wouldn't call it a full-time job or anything, but it's something I like to do on the side."

He went quiet for a minute, apparently doing his best to absorb everything I'd just said and stack it up against all the situations he'd seen or experienced while we were together. I had a feeling a lot of small details that had seemed sort of odd to him were now beginning to make a lot more sense.

Whether he'd be able to roll with it was still up for debate, though.

"And that woman who kidnapped me—"

"Is the witch who murdered Milton Keyes," I finished for him.

His expression had turned bleak again. "And that other woman...her sister...what exactly did she and the witch from your coven do to my kidnapper?"

Still not the easiest thing in the world to explain, but again, better than addressing the tension simmering between us.

"Magic resides in a witch's pineal gland," I said, knowing I sounded too pedantic, taking refuge in the careful words. "Elise learned a while back that there was a spell you could use to burn it out." I paused there and wondered if I should mention how we'd done the same thing to Tonya Willis, then decided to leave it alone. Better to focus on what had just happened to Larissa Richter.

"And that makes Larissa what...an ordinary person now?"

"Basically," I replied. "She won't remember being a witch. She won't believe that magic is real. I'm sure Melissa will plant the suggestion in her mind that she killed Milton because she was jealous of his relationship with her twin sister. It's not all that implausible."

Noah was quiet for a second or two, thoughts obviously churning away. While I doubted he liked the idea of someone being coerced into confession, it was also clear that he knew Larissa was guilty, and therefore should face whatever justice might be coming her to her.

"It's the easiest way to handle something like this," I told him. "We can't allow a witch who knows about the world of magic to enter the justice system, to be in a position to reveal things that should be hidden out of spite at the people who helped put her in prison. We have to keep our secrets."

"Back to that," Noah said, mouth tight.

Yes, we'd circled back to the one subject I really wished I could avoid. However, I knew we couldn't dance around the topic forever. Whatever happened, I had to tell Noah the truth.

"How do you think the world would react if people learned witches lived among them, that magic was real?" I asked. "Do you think they'd just shrug and say, 'Oh, that's interesting,' and then go on with their lives? I mean, think about the witch trials right here in Salem. Things didn't go so well for those women."

"That was a long time ago," Noah argued. "Things were different then."

"Not as different as you might think," I said. "People are still afraid of the unknown. And the thing is, the vast majority of us don't use our powers for anything terrible. I might stir a little magic into my insomnia elixir so it's more effective, and my mother might say a little charm every morning as she brushes her hair to keep the gray away. Things like that. But a lot of people won't believe we're harmless. They'll think we're all like Larissa Richter."

Noah was quiet again, brain clearly working furiously as he did his best to take in these additional pieces of information.

"When were you going to tell me?" he asked abruptly.

Now it was my turn to rub my damp palms against the knees of my jeans. Over and over, I'd thought, *I'll tell him after he tells me he loves me.* Or, even worse, *I'll tell him when he asks me to marry him.*

But how could I turn to him now and say that I'd been waiting for him to say those three all-important words? Even to me, that felt like a manipulation. Maybe not completely, but still, I'd been making my honesty about my witchy nature contingent on his words and actions, and I didn't know whether that was fair.

I was beginning to see why my mother had given up on finding her one true love and had decided to use artificial insemination to get the daughter she wanted. Right now, that scenario felt a whole lot less complicated.

About all I could do was shrug, which I could tell wasn't the correct response. Noah's jaw hardened, and it looked as though he was about to say something we'd both regret.

"I'm not being dismissive," I said quickly. "It's

different for each of us, deciding when to reveal such a huge secret. I suppose in our case I just wanted to give it a little more time."

There, that sounded honest enough without being too judge-y. The problem was, would Noah accept such an explanation?

Apparently not, because he retorted, "How much time? Were you going to go on hiding this huge secret for months? For years?"

Stung, I said, "I was waiting for you tell me you loved me!"

He stared at me, face blank. "You know I care for you," he said, his tone flat.

"I do," I said. "And I care for you. But we've been together for four months now, and neither one of us has said anything on the subject. No, we've just danced around it. In my case, I was only being careful because that's how I was raised. I *had* to be careful because I didn't have any other choice. What's your excuse?"

Those gorgeous blue eyes I loved so much narrowed. Then he rose slowly from the couch, saying, "I think maybe I need some time to figure this out."

He needed some time?

Wait...was he breaking up with me?

"Noah—" I said desperately, but he only shook his head.

"No, really," he cut in. "I've got to process all

this. But don't worry," he added, a bitter little smile pulling at his mouth. "I won't say a word to anyone. I mean, I'm sure you could probably cast a spell to shut me up if I started spreading your secrets around town, right?"

There was no real way for me to answer that question, not when I absolutely could cook up something to make sure Noah Jenkins never said a word about what he'd learned today. And if it turned out that I couldn't manage it for some reason, then I was sure someone else in my coven could.

"Just—just take the dogs and go home," he said, his tone almost gentle now. "I'll be in touch."

Could I even believe that he'd eventually reach out after he'd had time to think this all over? Or was he just saying something he knew would fend me off for a while?

I didn't want to answer either of those questions. Instead, I got up from my chair, said, "Okay," and left the living room, heading for the kitchen so I could call the dogs to me. They came at once, of course, their eyes full of questions, but I couldn't answer any of them now.

Maybe never.

In the meantime, there was only one thing I could do.

"Let's go home," I said.

The Familiar Spirits series concludes with *Runes and Ravens*.

Also by Christine Pope

THE DJINN WARS

(Paranormal Romance)

Chosen

Taken

Fallen

Broken

Forsaken

Forbidden

Awoken

Illuminated

Stolen

Forgotten

Driven

Unspoken

Hidden

Written

Given

Mistaken

FAMILIAR SPIRITS

(Cozy Mystery/Paranormal Romance)

Spells and Spaniels

Cauldrons and Cats

Hexes and Hedgehogs

Charms and Chihuahuas

Runes and Ravens

LATTES AND LEVITATION*

(Cozy Mystery/Paranormal Romance)

Caffeine Before Curses

Muffins After Magic

Pastries and Prophecies

Eclairs and Ectoplasm

Sugar Skulls and Specters

Wedding Cakes and Wishes

HEDGEWITCH FOR HIRE

(Cozy Mystery/Paranormal Romance)

Grave Mistake

Social Medium

Household Demons

Perpetual Potion

Jingle Spells

Wandering Monsters

Uninvited Ghosts

Prophet Motive

Ballroom Bits

Spell Check

Brew Confessions

Charm School

UNEXPECTED MAGIC*

(Urban Fantasy/Paranormal Romance)

Found Objects

Finders, Keepers

Lost and Found

Finding Destiny

THE WITCHES OF WHEELER PARK*

(Paranormal Romance)

Storm Born

Thunder Road

Winds of Change

Mind Games

A Wheeler Park Christmas

Blood Ties

Healing Hands

Wishful Thinking

Smoke and Mirrors

MISS PRIMM'S ACADEMY FOR WAYWARD WITCHES*

(Fantasy/Academy Romance)

Misspelled

Dispelled

Expelled

PROJECT DEMON HUNTERS*

(Paranormal Romance)

Unquiet Souls

Unbound Spirits

Unholy Ground

Unseen Voices

Unmarked Graves

Unbroken Vows

THE DEVIL YOU KNOW*

(Paranormal Romance)

Sympathy for the Devil

Charmed, I'm Sure

A Wing and a Prayer

Wish Upon a Star

THE WITCHES OF CANYON ROAD*

(Paranormal Romance)

Hidden Gifts

Darker Paths

Mysterious Ways

A Canyon Road Christmas

Demon Born

An Ill Wind

Higher Ground

Haunted Hearts

THE WITCHES OF CLEOPATRA HILL*

(Paranormal Romance)

Darkangel

Darknight

Darkmoon

Sympathetic Magic

Protector

Spellbound

A Cleopatra Hill Christmas

Impractical Magic

Strange Magic

The Arrangement

Defender

Bad Blood

Deep Magic

Darktide

THE WATCHERS TRILOGY*

(Paranormal Romance)

Falling Dark

Dead of Night

Rising Dawn

THE SEDONA FILES*

(Paranormal/Science Fiction Romance)

Bad Vibrations

Desert Hearts

Angel Fire

Star Crossed

Falling Angels

Enemy Mine

TALES OF THE LATTER KINGDOMS*

(Fantasy Romance)

All Fall Down

Dragon Rose

Binding Spell

Ashes of Roses

One Thousand Nights

Threads of Gold

The Wolf of Harrow Hall

Moon Dance

The Song of the Thrush

THE GAIAN CONSORTIUM SERIES*

(Science Fiction Romance)

Beast (free prequel novella)

Blood Will Tell

Breath of Life

The Gaia Gambit

The Mandala Maneuver

The Titan Trap

The Zhore Deception

The Refugee Ruse

STANDALONE TITLES

Hearts on Fire (Paranormal Romance)

Taking Dictation (Contemporary Romance)

Golden Heart (Gaslamp Fantasy Romance)

Night Music: A Modern Reimagining of The Phantom of the Opera (Contemporary Romance)

Ghost Dance: A Sequel to Gaston Leroux's The Phantom of the Opera (Historical Mystery/Romance)

Flight Before Christmas (Fantasy Romance)

* Indicates a completed series

About the Author

USA Today bestselling author Christine Pope has been writing stories ever since she commandeered her family's Smith-Corona typewriter back in grade school. Her work includes paranormal romance, cozy paranormal mystery, and urban fantasy, among others. She makes her home in Arizona.

Christine Pope on the Web:
www.christinepope.com

facebook.com/ChristinePopeAuthor
pinterest.com/ChristineJPope
bookbub.com/authors/christine-pope

www.ingramcontent.com/pod-product-compliance
Lightning Source LLC
LaVergne TN
LVHW091114080826
845145LV00008B/1913

* 9 7 8 1 9 4 6 4 3 5 7 2 9 *